D0103012

LONG
TIME
COMING

Sandra Brown

BANTAM BOOKS

LONG TIME COMING
A Bantam Book

PUBLISHING HISTORY
Doubleday Loveswept edition published January 1989
Bantam mass market edition / January 1994
Bantam hardcover reissue / January 2006

Published by Bantam Dell
A Division of Random House, Inc.
New York, New York

This is a work of fiction. Names, characters, places, and incidents either are the product of the author's imagination or are used fictitiously. Any resemblance to actual persons, living or dead, events, or locales is entirely coincidental.

Book design by Robert Bull

Bantam Books is a registered trademark of Random House, Inc., and the colophon is a trademark of Random House, Inc.

ISBN-13: 978-0-553-80409-6
ISBN-10: 0-553-80409-X

Printed in the United States of America

Dear Reader,

You have my wholehearted thanks for the interest and enthusiasm you've shown for my Loveswept romances over the past decade. I'm enormously pleased that the enjoyment I derived from writing them was contagious. Obviously you share my fondness for love stories that always end happily and leave us with a warm inner glow.

Nothing quite equals the excitement one experiences when falling in love. In each romance, I tried to capture that excitement. The settings and characters and plots changed, but that was the recurring theme.

Something in all of us delights in lovers and their uneven pursuit of fulfillment and happiness. Indeed, the pursuit is half the fun! I became deeply involved with each pair of lovers and their unique story. As though paying a visit to old friends for whom I played matchmaker, I often reread their stories myself.

I hope you enjoy this encore edition of one of my personal favorites.

—SANDRA BROWN

LONG
TIME
COMING

1

The Porsche crept along the street like a sleek black panther. Hugging the curb, its engine purred so deep and low it sounded like a predator's growl.

Marnie Hibbs was kneeling in the fertile soil of her flower bed, digging among the impatiens under the ligustrum bushes and cursing the little bugs that made three meals a day of them, when the sound of the car's motor attracted her attention. She glanced at it over her shoulder, then panicked as it came to a stop in front of her house.

"Lord, is it that late?" she muttered. Dropping her trowel, she stood up and brushed the clinging damp earth off her bare knees.

She reached up to push her dark bangs off her forehead before she realized that she still had on her heavy gardening gloves. Quickly she peeled them off and dropped them beside the trowel, all the while watching the driver get out of the sports car and start up her front walk.

Glancing at her wristwatch, she saw that she hadn't lost track of time. He was just very early for their appointment, and as a result, she wasn't going to make a very good first impression. Being hot, sweaty, and dirty was no way to meet a client. And she needed this commission badly.

Forcing a smile, she moved down the sidewalk to greet him, nervously trying to remember if she had left the house and studio reasonably neat when she decided to do an hour's worth of yard work. She had planned to tidy up before he arrived.

She might look like the devil, but she didn't want to appear intimidated. Self-confident friendliness was the only way to combat the disadvantage of having been caught looking her worst.

He was still several yards away from her when she greeted him. "Hello," she said with a bright smile. "Obviously we got our signals switched. I thought you weren't coming until later."

"I decided this diabolical game of yours had gone on long enough."

Marnie's sneakers skidded on the old concrete walk as she came to an abrupt halt. She tilted her head in stunned surprise. "I'm sorry, I—"

"Who the hell are you, lady?"

"Miss Hibbs. Who do you think?"

"Never heard of you. Just what the devil are you up to?"

"Up to?" She glanced around helplessly, as though the giant sycamores in her front yard might provide an answer to this bizarre interrogation.

"Why've you been sending me those letters?"

"Letters?"

He was clearly furious, and her lack of comprehension only seemed to make him angrier. He bore down on her like a hawk on a field mouse, until she had to bow her back to look up at him. The summer sun was behind him, casting him in silhouette.

He was blond, tall, trim, and dressed in casual slacks and a sport shirt—all stylish, impeccably so. He was wearing opaque aviator glasses, so she couldn't see his eyes, but if they were as belligerent as his expression and stance, she was better off not seeing them.

"I don't know what you're talking about."

"The letters, lady, the letters." He strained the words through a set of strong white teeth.

"*What* letters?"

"Don't play dumb."

"Are you sure you've got the right house?"

He took another step forward. "I've got the right house," he said in a voice that was little more than a snarl.

"Obviously you don't." She didn't like being put on the defensive, especially by someone she'd never met over something of which she was totally ignorant. "You're either crazy or drunk, but in any case, you're *wrong*. I'm not the person you're looking for and I demand that you leave my property. Now."

"You were expecting me. I could tell by the way you spoke to me."

"I thought you were the man from the advertising agency."

"Well, I'm not."

"Thank God." She would hate having to do business with someone this irrational and ill-tempered.

"You know damn well who I am," he said, peeling off the sunglasses.

Marnie sucked in a quick, sharp breath and fell back a step because she did indeed know who he was. She raised a hand to her chest in an attempt at keeping her jumping heart in place. "Law," she gasped.

"That's right. Law Kincaid. Just like you wrote it on the envelopes."

She was shocked to see him after all these years, standing only inches in front of her. This time he wasn't merely a familiar image in the newspaper or on her television screen. He was flesh and blood. The years had been kind to that flesh, improving his looks, not eroding them.

She wanted to stand and stare, but he was staring at her with unmitigated contempt and no recognition at all. "Let's go inside, Mr. Kincaid," she suggested softly.

Several of her neighbors, who had been taking advantage of the sunny weekend weather to do yard chores, had stopped moving, edging, and watering to gawk at the car and Miss Hibbs's visitor.

It wasn't out of the ordinary for a man to come to her house. Many of her clients were men and most of them consulted with her there. Generally they were stodgy executives in dark business suits. Few had deep tans, looked like movie stars, and drove such ostentatious cars.

This area of Houston wasn't glitzy like some of the newer neighborhoods. Most of the residents were middle-aged and drove sensible sedans. A Porsche on the block was a curious thing indeed. And to her neighbors' recollections, Marnie Hibbs had never engaged in a shouting match with anyone.

She turned on the squeaky rubber soles of her sneakers and led Law Kincaid up the sidewalk and through the front door of her house. Air-conditioning was a welcome respite from the humidity outside, but since she was damp with perspiration, the colder air chilled her. Or maybe it was her distinct awareness of the man behind her that was giving her goose bumps.

"This way."

She led him down a spacious hallway, the kind that could be found only in houses built before World War II, and toward the glassed-in back porch, which served as her studio. There she felt more at home, more at ease, and better able to deal with the astonishing reality that Law Kincaid had unexpectedly walked into her life again.

When she turned to face him, his arctic-blue eyes were

darting around the studio. They connected with hers like magnets.

"Well?" he said tersely, placing his hands on his hips. He was obviously awaiting a full explanation for something Marnie was in the dark about herself.

"I don't know anything about any letters, Mr. Kincaid."

"They were mailed from this address."

"Then there's been a mistake at the post office."

"Unlikely. Not five times over the course of several weeks. Look, Mrs. uh . . . what was it again?"

"Hibbs. Miss Hibbs."

He gave her a swift, inquisitive once-over. "*Miss* Hibbs, I've been a bachelor for thirty-nine years. It's been a while since puberty. I don't remember every woman I've gone to bed with."

Her heart did another little dance number, and she took a quick, insufficient breath. "I've never been to bed with you."

He threw one hip slightly off-center and cocked his head arrogantly. "Then how is it that you claim to have mothered a son by me? A son I'd never even heard of until I got your first letter several weeks ago."

Marnie stared at him with speechless dismay. She could feel the color draining from her face. It felt like the world had been yanked from beneath her feet.

"I've never had a child. And I repeat, I never sent you a letter." She gestured at a chair. "Why don't you sit down?" She didn't offer him a seat out of courtesy or any concern for his comfort. She was afraid that if she didn't sit, and soon, her knees would buckle beneath her.

He thought about it for a moment, gnawing irritably on the corner of his lower lip before he moved to a rattan chair. He sat down on the very edge of the cushion, as though wanting to be ready to spring off it if the need arose.

Self-conscious of her muddy sneakers, ragged cutoffs, and ancient T-shirt, Marnie sat in the matching chair facing his. She sat straight, keeping her dirty knees together and clasping her hands nervously on the tops of her thighs.

She felt unclothed and vulnerable as his incisive eyes moved over her, taking in her face, her uncombed hair, her yard work attire, and her grubby knees.

"You recognized me." He shot the sentence at her like a missile.

"Anybody who watches TV or reads a newspaper would recognize you. You're the most popular astronaut since John Glenn."

"And therefore I'm a visible target for every nutcase who comes down the pike."

"I am not a nutcase!"

"Then why the hell have you been sending me those letters? That's not even an original idea, you know. I get several dozen a day."

"Congratulations."

"They're not all fan letters. Some are hate mail from the religious crazies who believe we're going where God never intended man to go. Some credit God with the *Challenger* accident—His punishment for our tampering with heaven or nonsense to that effect. I've had proposals of marriage and of other assorted liaisons of a prurient and/or perverted nature," he said dryly.

"How nice for you."

Ignoring her snide remark, he continued. "But your letters had a stroke of originality. You were the first one to claim that I was the father of your child."

"Don't you listen? I told you I've never had a child. How could you possibly be the father?"

"My point exactly, Miss Hibbs!" he shouted.

Marnie stood. So did he. He tracked her when she moved to her drafting table and needlessly began rearranging sketch pencils and paintbrushes in their various canisters.

"You were also the first one to threaten me with public exposure if I didn't do what you wanted me to."

She turned to find him very close. She could even feel the fabric of his trousers against her bare legs. "What possible threat could *I* pose to you? You're the fair-haired child of the space program, hailed as a hero. You held every American spellbound in front of his television set while you and a Russian cosmonaut shook hands over a peace treaty in space.

"There was a ticker-tape parade in honor of you and your crew in New York. You had dinner at the White House with the President and First Lady. Almost single-handedly you've turned around public opinion on NASA, which certainly wasn't favorable after *Challenger*. Critics of manned spaceflight are being ridiculed after what you've done.

"To pit little ol' me against a celebrity giant like you, I would have to be crazy or stupid. I assure you that I'm neither."

"You called me Law."

After her lengthy speech, his four-word rebuttal came as an anticlimax that took her off guard. "What?"

"When you first recognized me, you called me Law."

"Which happens to be your name."

"But the average man on the street would address me as Colonel Kincaid, nothing as familiar as Law. Unless we'd known each other well before."

She sidestepped that. "What did these alleged letters demand from you?"

"Money first."

"Money?" she exclaimed. "How crass."

"Followed by public acknowledgment of my son."

Marnie eased herself from between him and the drafting table. His closeness was wreaking havoc on her ability to think clearly. She began shuffling through a stack of sketches left lying on one of her worktables. "I'm a very independent, self-reliant person. I would never ask you or anybody else for money."

"This is a nice neighborhood, a big house."

"My parents'."

"They live here with you?"

"No. My father is dead. My mother suffered a stroke several months ago and is in a rest home." She slapped down the stack of sketches and faced him. "I manage to support myself. What business of yours is any of this?"

"I think the victim ought to get to know his extortioner." Huskily he added, "In every way."

His eyes moved over her again. This time more slowly and analytically. She saw them pause in the vicinity of her breasts, which the damp T-shirt did little to conceal. She could feel her nipples projecting against the worn, soft cotton and tried unsuccessfully to convince herself that the response resulted from the air-conditioning, and not Law Kincaid's stare.

"I'm afraid you'll have to excuse me now," she said with affected haughtiness. "I'm expecting someone soon and I've got to clean up."

"Who are you expecting? The agency man?" At her startled expression, he said, "You mentioned him when I first got here."

"He has an appointment to look at my proposed sketches for a commission."

"You're an artist?"

"An illustrator."

"For whom?"

"For myself. I freelance."

"What project are you working on?"

"The cover of the Houston telephone directory."

His tawny eyebrows rose a fraction, impressed. "That's quite a commission."

"I haven't gotten it yet." Marnie could have bitten her tongue the minute the words were out. He was shrewd enough to catch the slip.

"It would be an important commission to you?"

"Of course. Now, if you'll—"

He caught her arm as she tried to go around him, headed for the front door. "It must get tough, living from one commission to the next while you maintain this house and pay your sick mother's medical bills."

"I do fine."

"But you're not rich."

"Not by a long shot."

"That's why you've been writing me these threatening letters, isn't it? To get money from me?"

"No. For the umpteenth time, I haven't ever written you a letter."

"Blackmail's a serious crime, Miss Hibbs."

"And a charge too ridiculous even to discuss. Now, please let go of my arm."

He wasn't hurting her. But his encircling fingers held her much too close to him. She was close enough to smell his sexy cologne and the minty freshness of his breath, close enough to see the dark centers of eyes that had sold more copies of *Time* than any other issue in history when they'd graced the front cover.

"You seem reasonably intelligent," he said.

"Should I take that as a compliment?"

"So why did you send anonymous letters to me, then put your return address on the envelope?"

She gave a soft, disbelieving laugh and shook her head. "I didn't. Or was that a trick question designed to trap me? Where are these letters? May I see them? Perhaps after I saw them I could offer an explanation."

"Do I look stupid? I wouldn't hand them over to you so you could destroy the evidence."

"Oh, for heaven's sake," she cried. Then, staring up into his stern face, she said, "You're really taking this seriously, aren't you?"

"At first I didn't. You were just one crank in hundreds. But after the fifth letter, when you got really nasty about pinning a paternity rap on me, I thought it was time to confront you."

"I'm not the kind of woman who would pin a paternity rap on any man."

"Even one with as high a public profile as me?"

"No."

"One who stood to lose a lot if there was a scandal?"

"That's right! Besides, I've told you that I've never had a child."

They heard the front door open, then bang shut. There were running steps in the hall. Then a tall, lanky teenage boy rushed through the door.

"Mom, you gotta come see the car parked in front of our house. It's totally *bad*!"

During the ponderous silence, Marnie listened to the knocking of her own heart. She tried to keep her face composed for the boy's sake, but it was difficult. After several seconds she hazarded a glance at Law Kincaid. He was staring at David. Disbelief was starkly evident on his handsome features.

It was David who finally spoke. "Jeez, you're Law Kincaid. Jeez!"

"David, I've asked you not to use that word."

"Sorry, Mom, but it's *Law Kincaid*. Law Kincaid in *my* house."

The astronaut replaced the incredulous expression on his face with his famous smile, his equanimity apparently regained. "David? Pleased to meet you." He stepped forward and shook the teenager's hand.

Across the room, Marnie gripped the edge of her

drafting table for support. David was almost as tall as Law. His hair was the identical shade of blond, his eyes just as blue. He hadn't grown into his bones yet. They poked out like arrow tips at the shoulders, elbows, and ankles. Eventually, however, he would. The genetic blueprint had been drawn at conception. To know how he would look in twenty-two years, all David had to do was examine the man shaking hands with him.

Fortunately David was so starstruck to find the astronaut under his roof that he didn't notice the resemblance. Exuberantly he pumped Law's hand.

"I've got posters of the *Victory* in my room. Burger King was giving them away if you bought six Whoppers. I bought seven just in case. Would you autograph it for me? I can't believe this. What are you doing here? My birthday's still weeks away."

He looked at Marnie and laughed. "Is this the special present you've been hinting at? Oh, wait, I know. Did you talk him into posing? That's it, right?"

Law turned his back to the boy and faced her. His stare was as hot and blue as a flame. She quailed beneath it but kept her expression defiant. Law's expression was a mix of suspicion and puzzlement. "Posing?"

"I . . . I . . ."

"Uh-oh, did I let the cat out of the bag before she had a chance to ask you? Sorry, Mom." To Law, David said, "She's making a pitch to do the cover of the phone book.

The other night she said she ought to get you to pose for the astronaut representing NASA."

"Hmm. Did she say why?"

"She thinks you're the best-looking, I guess," David said, grinning. "She knows you're the most famous."

"I see," Law said quietly. "I'm flattered."

"Will you do it?"

Law mercifully released Marnie from his stare and turned back to David. "Sure I'll pose. Why not?"

"Gee, that's terrific."

"It really isn't necessary," Marnie interjected. "I've already done a preliminary sketch." She gestured noncommittally toward the stack of sketches behind her.

"Let's see them."

"They're not ready for anybody to see."

"Don't you plan to show them to the adman?"

"Yes, but he's in the business. He knows the difference between a rough sketch and the finished product."

"So do I. And I'd like to see them." Law was issuing her a challenge. Aware of David's curious eyes and knowing how perceptive he was, Marnie had no choice but to go along.

"Okay, sure." In contrast to her congenial voice, her smile felt brittle and breakable as she passed some of the sketches to Law.

"See, there you are!" David exclaimed, pointing down at the man's face in the montage of scenes depicting Houston. "Looks just like you, doesn't it?"

"It certainly does," Law said, giving Marnie another of those penetrating, inquiring stares. "Almost as though she knew my face intimately."

"She's good. The best," David boasted. "She even got the space suit right."

Marnie snatched the drawings back. "Since my drawings meet with your approval, there's really no reason for me to detain you, Colonel Kincaid. Thank you so much for stopping—"

The doorbell cut her off.

"I'll get it," David shouted, tearing off in that direction. Before he'd taken two steps, however, he braked and spun around. "You won't leave before I get back, will you?"

"No," Law told him. "I'll be here for a while."

"Great!"

The boy bounded down the hallway toward the front of the house, where the doorbell was being rung a second time.

Law closed in on Marnie and took her by both arms. In hushed but angry tones he hissed, "I thought you said you'd never had a son."

"I haven't."

"What do you call that?"

"I'm not his mother."

"He calls you mom."

"Yes, but—"

"And he resembles me."

"He—"

"But, dammit, I don't remember sleeping with you."

"You didn't! You didn't remember me on sight, did you?"

"Not on sight. But some things I never forget."

He yanked her hard against him. Before she could react, his lips were working hers open. His tongue breached them and dipped into her mouth. Opening his hand wide across her bottom, he tilted her hips forward and up against his.

A geyser of desire shot through Marnie.

Apparently Law was likewise struck.

His head snapped up and he looked at her with frank astonishment before pushing her away.

It all transpired within a matter of seconds, which was good since David was leading her most potentially important client to date down the hallway toward the studio.

By the time they reached it, Law was lounging against the edge of her desk, looking as innocent as a choirboy. She was standing in the middle of the room, feeling as adrift as if she were in the middle of the Pacific without a life raft.

"Mr. Howard," she said breathlessly, her fingertips on her throbbing lips, "please forgive my appearance. I was working in the yard when . . ." She gestured toward Law. "When Colonel Kincaid surprised us by stopping by."

She needn't have worried about him being put off by her disheveled appearance. He didn't even notice her. "Well, this is certainly an unexpected pleasure," he said expansively. The advertising agency executive stepped forward to shake the astronaut's hand. "It's an honor, sir."

"Thank you."

Only then did he acknowledge Marnie. "Ms. Hibbs, you didn't tell me you knew our latest national hero." Law's brows drew together into a frown. Clearing his throat uncomfortably, the man added, "No reason you should, of course."

"Colonel Kincaid's the model for her sketch for the phone book."

"*If* I get the job, David," she said, self-consciously wetting her lips. She tasted Law's kiss on them and experienced the outlandish but not unfounded fear that it might be visible. "Would you like to see the drawings I've made so far, Mr. Howard?"

"While you're doing that," Law said, "I'm going to take David for a drive."

"You mean in the Porsche?" the boy asked ecstatically. He let out an Indian war cry, leapt in the air, slapped the ceiling, and then raced from the room. "I've got my learner's permit, you know," he called back. "I'll get my license in just a few more weeks."

"David, don't you dare touch Colonel Kincaid's car," Marnie cried in alarm.

"He'll be all right."

"But where are you going?"

"Around the block," he said, giving a casual shrug with one shoulder. "No place special."

"How long will you be gone?"

"Awhile."

She wanted to scream at him for giving her vague answers. She wanted to put her foot down and say no, definitely not, David wasn't going anywhere with him. She wanted to run after David and grab hold tightly.

But with Mr. Howard standing there, she had no alternative but to be gracious. Knowing that, Law took full advantage of the situation. She watched him swagger down the hallway and out the front door to meet David, who was already sitting in the passenger seat of the car.

"Have you, uh, known Colonel Kincaid long?" Mr. Howard asked tentatively.

Marnie turned and saw that the man was dying of curiosity. He didn't have the nerve to come right out and ask about the relationship between the astronaut and the teenager who called her mom. Coolly she replied, "I've known him awhile."

Mr. Howard left twenty minutes later. She felt confident that he liked her preliminary sketches. He warned her, however, as he was zipping them into a large portfolio, that there were two other artists being considered and that the final decision would be left up to a committee of agency and telephone company executives.

"Your work is more avant garde than the other two."

"Is that bad?"

"No," he replied with a smile. "Maybe it's time we broke with the traditional." Beyond that all he would say was, "You'll be hearing from us one way or the other in a week or so."

She walked him to the front door. Through the screen she watched him leave, at the same time scanning the street for a sign of the Porsche. It was nowhere in sight. Worriedly she wrung her hands. Where had they gone? What were they talking about? Was Law barraging David with questions he wouldn't know the answers to?

Before she worked herself into a tizzy, she decided to take a long-overdue shower. Shortly she emerged from her second story bedroom dressed, wearing makeup, and feeling more self-assured than she had in cutoffs and T-shirt.

She was relieved to hear voices coming from David's bedroom. Stepping through the open doorway, she saw him listening, enthralled, to Law's description of the walk he'd taken in space.

"Weren't you scared?" David asked.

"No. By the time we got up there, we'd rehearsed everything so many times, I knew exactly what to expect."

"But something could have gone wrong."

"It could have. But I knew that I had a crew in the ship and another on the ground making sure that nothing did."

"What's it like when you blast off?"

Law squeezed his eyes shut. "Thrilling. Like nothing else. It's the culmination of tedious hard work, study, practice, delays, decision-making. But it's worth every second of the anticipation and frustration. More."

David inched closer. "What were you thinking?"

"Honestly?"

"Honestly."

"I was praying I wouldn't overflow my tee-tee bag."

David laughed. "No. Really?"

"Well, besides that, I was thinking, 'This is it. This is what I've always wanted to do. This is what I was born for. It's here. I'm living it.' "

"Gee."

The worshipful look on his face alarmed Marnie. "I hate to break this up," she said from the doorway, "but I've got to go to the rest home now. And, David, if you don't leave soon, you'll be late for soccer practice."

David rolled off his bed and landed on his feet. "Mom, you'll never believe this! He let me drive! That car is something else, almost like being in a cockpit, isn't it, Colonel Kincaid?"

"Almost. That's why I bought it. If I can't be flying, I want to pretend I am."

"It was terrific, Mom. You should've been with us." Then, looking guilty for being so caught up in his own excitement, he asked, "How'd your meeting with Mr. Howard go?"

"He liked my rough sketches but made no promises." Needlessly she consulted her wristwatch. "You'd better go, David."

"You play soccer?" Law had been sitting on the edge of David's bed. He came to his feet.

"I'm a halfback for the Tornadoes, my school team. We're going to be city champs."

"I like that tone of confidence," Law said with a broad smile.

"To make sure we win, the coach is working us double time."

"Then you'd better not be late for practice." They moved toward the door where Marnie was waiting.

"Will you be here when I get back?"

"No, he won't." When Marnie curtly answered the question that had been intended for Law, four identical eyes were turned on her. She gave a weak smile. "I'm sure Colonel Kincaid has other things to do, David. Run along now. But be careful on your bike. Got your house key?"

"Yes, Mom. Well, 'bye, Colonel Kincaid. I can't believe I got to meet you. Thanks for autographing my poster."

"It was my pleasure, David." They shook hands. For the first time that Marnie could ever remember, David seemed reluctant to go to soccer practice.

He trudged down the stairs, frequently turning his head to gaze back at Law. As soon as he was out the front door, Marnie looked up at her visitor.

"I really do need to leave for the rest home now. My mother's not doing well, and if I'm not there when she expects me, she—"

He blocked her path and checked the flow of superfluous words. The charm he had turned on for David had disappeared with the boy. "I want the truth from you. I want it now." He took a quick breath. "Is he my son?"

Her gray eyes filled with tears. Her tongue made a swipe

at the lips now shiny with peach-colored gloss. She bowed her dark head so that the crown of soft curls almost touched the center of his chest.

"He's *my* son," she whispered. *"Mine."*

"Somebody fathered him." Crooking a finger beneath her chin, he tilted her head up. "Is he my son?"

Marnie looked directly into his eyes and answered, "Yes."

3

He encircled her upper arm with his hand. "I'll drive you wherever you need to go."

"You'll do no such thing."

"We need to talk."

"There's nothing to talk about."

"Like hell," he said, lowering his face to inches above hers. "You just told me I've got a teenage son. One million would be a conservative estimate of how many questions I've got to ask you. Until I get some answers, I'm sticking to you like glue. Now, for the final time, I'll drive," he concluded emphatically.

Marnie would have rebelled, but he had a death grip on her arm as they went downstairs. It would have been foolish to engage in a tug-of-war she couldn't possibly win. Then, too, she reasoned that he was due an explanation.

Her dignity was tinged with hauteur, but she went peaceably.

"Lock your door," Law told her. "Don't you have a burglar alarm system?"

"No."

"You should. This is a large house with lots of ways for a thief to break in."

He ushered her through her front door and down the sidewalk to his waiting Porsche. Once she was situated in the passenger seat, he went around the low, long hood and slid behind the steering wheel.

"Where to?"

She gave him the name of the street along with the expressway exit to take. Within minutes they were speeding down the inside lane of the freeway. Marnie gripped the edge of her seat. He drove as though he were strapped inside a rocket. It didn't help her nerves to notice that his eyes spent more time on her than on the road.

Having tolerated that keen stare for as long as she could, she demanded, "What are you staring at?"

"You. You're so tiny. You don't look like you could carry a child. And"—he shook his head in bafflement—"it confounds me that I don't remember sleeping with you."

His eyes dropped to her mouth, then to the slender column of her neck, then to her chest, finally to her lap. His intensity made her feel naked. She was tempted to cover herself with her hands.

"I must've been real drunk," he said roughly. "Otherwise I think I would remember having sex with you."

"I've never had . . . I've never slept with you." She kept her head straight and stared through the tinted windshield, finding it unnerving to make eye contact with him and thinking that at least one of them should be watching the road. "David isn't my son."

"Then—"

"He's my sister's child. You and she . . ." She shrugged awkwardly and gave him a quick glance and a tepid smile. "It's the next exit. You'd better get in the other lane."

He did, whipping in front of a bakery truck. The driver sat on his horn and shouted an obscenity. The stop sign at the bottom of the ramp hardly gave Law pause before he took the turn in third gear.

"Your sister supposedly got pregnant by me, right?"

"Not supposedly. She did. It was a summer romance."

"What summer?"

"You had just graduated from the Naval Academy and were about to go on active duty."

He instantly became defensive and belligerent. "How do you know David's mine?" She shot him a withering glance. "Okay, okay, he looks like me a little, I'll admit. But that doesn't prove anything."

"I don't have to prove it," she retorted. "It makes no difference to me whether you believe it or not. Turn right at the corner."

He impatiently waited for the signal light to change, then went through it like a bronco out of the chute. "There's the rest home," she said gratefully when they were still a block away. It would take him at least that far to reduce his speed enough to turn into the drive.

"You can drop me at that side door. I've got a key so I can let myself in to see her at any time."

It was a small church-supported facility with lovely grounds and a highly qualified staff. Mrs. Hibbs's stroke hadn't left her completely paralyzed, but disabled enough to require round-the-clock nursing. Moving her out of the house had been a heartbreaking decision for Marnie, especially knowing that her mother would never leave the rest home alive.

It had been even more difficult for Marnie to admit how much strain had been relieved when her mother left the house. For the last several years her mother had become increasingly bitter and impossible to please.

When Law brought his car to a stop at the private side entrance, Marnie opened the door and placed one foot on the pavement. She spoke to him over her shoulder.

"I don't know who sent you those letters telling you about David, but they did not come from me. I never intended for you to know about him or vice-versa. I don't want anything from you, especially money. So just go on about your business, leave me to mine, and forget that today ever happened. Thank you for the ride."

She got out. At the door of the hospital, while she fumbled with the lock that she usually opened so deftly, she wanted to turn and take a final, long look at him.

It had been seventeen years since she'd last seen him. He'd waved them good-bye, then turned and jogged down the beach, looking like a young, vibrant sun god, golden and beautiful and destined for fame.

Her breaking heart had said a secret good-bye to him then. She didn't now. She didn't allow herself the luxury of looking back before entering the sterile building.

She remained in her mother's room for over an hour. During most of that time Mrs. Hibbs slept, waking up only occasionally to speak a few slurred sentences to Marnie.

Despondent, Marnie left her. When she came out of the room, Law was pacing the hallway. The nurses at the station at the end of the hall were all atwitter, but he was paying attention to nothing save the gleaming tile floor as he walked to and fro like a caged lion.

"You're still here?" Marnie asked. She was already feeling emotionally raw after the visit at her mother's bedside. Seeing Law upset her further.

"How were you planning to get home?"

"Taxi."

He shook his head and escorted her to the nearest exit. "Taxis are unreliable in this town. You ought to know that." Minutes later they were once again in his Porsche with only the console and seventeen years between them.

"How is your mother?"

"She's dying."

After a respectful pause he said, "I'm sorry."

"They keep her medicated to minimize the damage of the little strokes she continues to have. Most of the time she's groggy. When she's lucid, she talks about my father and Sharon. She also cries a lot."

"It was in Galveston, wasn't it?"

"You mean when we met?"

"It was on the beach, right?"

"Yes," she said, wondering how much he remembered. "My family was renting a beach house close to the one your family was renting."

Squinting through the windshield, he murmured, "There were two of you. Sisters."

"My older sister, Sharon, and me, Marnie."

"Sharon and Marnie. Yeah, I've got it now. Your sister was quite a looker."

Marnie ducked her head slightly. "That's right."

"You were just a kid."

"Fourteen."

"And your daddy was a preacher, wasn't he? I remember we had to sneak off to drink beer."

"You talked Sharon into drinking some."

He laughed. "But you wouldn't. Goody-two-shoes she called you."

"I was never as adventurous as Sharon."

He contemplated that for a moment, then remarked, "If

Sharon slept with me, she probably slept with dozens of other guys."

"She was only sixteen that summer. You were her first."

"Sixteen? *Sixteen?*" he repeated, his face going ashen. "I thought she was older than sixteen."

"She looked older," Marnie said in a low voice.

"She sure as hell did. Acted older too. Her attitude had left sixteen behind long before I met her. I remember how well she filled out the top of her bikini. She sure as hell didn't have a teenager's body."

"I'm not arguing that," Marnie snapped. Irrationally it annoyed her that he remembered how well-endowed Sharon was. It didn't surprise her, of course, she just wished he'd stop referring to it.

"But that's how old she was, sixteen. And turning up pregnant the first week of your junior year in high school can have grave repercussions, especially if your father happens to be a well-known minister in the community."

Law turned into the parking lot of a brightly lit coffee shop. "You look like you could use something to drink."

"I'd rather you take me home."

"Look," he said with diminishing patience, "you're shaken and upset. Wouldn't a Coke or a cup of coffee do you some good? For heaven's sake, I'm not asking you to get drunk or spend the night with me. Are you still such a goody-two-shoes that you can't have coffee with a man?"

Without waiting for her answer, he got out, slamming

the car door behind him. He came around for her. She watched eyes light up with recognition as the hostess led them to a booth. Whispers and soft exclamations of surprise and delight followed them like a wake. Self-consciously she slid into the booth.

"Does that happen everywhere you go?"

"What?" He looked at her with perplexity. "Oh, you mean the celebrity bit? Ignore it."

She tried, but it wasn't easy to do since she was getting as close a scrutiny as Law was. When the waitress approached with menus, she asked for Law's autograph, which he gave her along with their order for two cups of coffee.

"So what'd she do?" he asked as soon as the swooning waitress had withdrawn.

"Who?"

"Your sister. Sharon. What did she do when she learned she was pregnant?"

"Oh, she, uh . . ." Marnie lowered her eyes. "She wanted to have an abortion."

Across the table she sensed Law's reaction. His body got tense. She saw his hands form fists. It gratified her to know that Sharon's first option was as repugnant to Law as it had been to her. At least he hadn't been cavalier about it.

"Why didn't she?" he asked.

This was difficult for Marnie to discuss. It had been one

of the most tumultuous times within her family. That's when it had begun to disintegrate. None of them had ever been the same after it.

"Sharon confided her plans to me," Marnie told him in a small voice. "One night after supper Sharon said she needed to talk to me. She told me she was pregnant. She was scared. That frightened me because I'd never seen her that disturbed over anything before.

"We stayed up all night, crying together, wondering what we should do. Tracking you down was out of the question. You were in the navy and, well, we didn't think you'd care to know. We didn't know what to do.

"But I couldn't believe that she wanted to get rid of it, dispose of it like garbage. I mean, it was a baby, *your* baby." She paused, glanced at him, then went on.

"I couldn't stand the thought of it. And I knew that Mother and Dad would rather have an illegitimate child than an abortion on their consciences."

"So you told them what she intended to do," he said.

"Yes. They forbade her to. She was furious with all of us. Her nine months of pregnancy weren't very joyous. But then David was born," she added with a wistful smile, "and we all loved him."

"Even Sharon?"

Her smile faltered. "She came to love him. He was so adorable and precocious, it was impossible not to."

He stared at her, sensing there was more to tell, but the arrival of their coffee spared her from having to elaborate.

When the waitress withdrew, Law asked, "Why isn't David with Sharon now?"

"Sharon died." Wordlessly he stared at her. "When David was only four."

He took a sip of coffee. "How?"

"A car accident. My parents were devastated. Dad had a heart attack and died that same year. It's been just Mother, David, and me since then."

"That summer changed the course of your lives."

"I guess you could say that, yes," she agreed ruefully.

"That was a terrific summer for me. My folks wanted to treat me to a good time."

"I remember them. It was easy to see that they were very proud of you. You'd graduated at the top of your class. By the way, congratulations on realizing your goal and becoming an astronaut."

"How did you know that was my goal?"

"You told me. One afternoon while Sharon was sunbathing, you and I took an inner tube out to ride the waves. You told me then that you were going to navy flight school to become a test pilot, then you wanted to apply for the astronaut program. I was so proud when I read in the newspaper that you'd been accepted. I felt like . . . well, like I knew you."

He was smiling, but suddenly his smile disappeared. "I hadn't thought about that summer in Galveston for years. Hell of a way to be reminded," he grumbled, signaling the waitress to refill their coffee cups.

Marnie took a careful sip of hers, still mindful of the watching eyes of the customers all around them.

"I always wear a rubber."

Scalding coffee sloshed over her hand, burning it and flooding the saucer. She gasped. "I beg your pardon?"

He calmly plucked two napkins from the dispenser on the table and used them to soak up the brown lake in her saucer. "Did you burn your hand?"

"It's fine," she lied, wondering if she dared ask the waitress for butter. She didn't have to. Law waved her over and asked for some.

"No, it's fine, really," Marnie protested when the waitress promptly returned with a plate bearing a slab of butter the size of Rhode Island for Law Kincaid's clumsy date who had spilled coffee on her hand.

"Thanks," he told the waitress with a smile meant to dismiss her.

"I can do it," Marnie said. "Really, such a fuss over—"

"Give me your hand."

She stuck out her red, stinging hand. With two fingers he scooped up a glob of butter and smoothed it over the burn.

"Whenever I sleep with a woman, I use a condom," he said in a low voice. "Without fail."

His fingers slid between two of hers, smearing the creamy butter into the highly sensitive groove. Marnie nearly came off the booth's vinyl bench.

"The surgeon general would commend you."

Her voice didn't sound normal at all. The burn had caused it to go husky and rough. Either that, or Law's touch had. As his fingers continued to slide between hers, she squirmed on her seat and rolled her lips inward to keep from making small whimpers of pleasure. His touch also elicited a fluttering sensation in her lower body and a tingling in her breasts, especially at their centers.

"I was with Sharon before anybody ever heard of AIDS," he was saying. "I've always used condoms to prevent pregnancy. I wouldn't have had sex with a girl I met on the Galveston beach without wearing one."

His hand massage was too wonderful. It was about to liquefy Marnie with the ease that their combined body heat was melting the butter into her skin. Regretfully she pulled her hand out of his reach.

"Then you're still not convinced that David is your son."

"Be fair," he said, leaning across the table. "I didn't even know he existed before today. Do you expect me to blindly accept your explanations as fact?"

"I don't expect anything from you, Colonel Kincaid," she said frostily. "I told you that at the door of the hospital."

"Well, I'm not the kind of man who can shrug off even the possibility that I fathered a child. Granted I might get testy, because this is a real shocker. So indulge me. Let me ask a few questions and give me straight answers."

She moved her cup and saucer aside and propped her

forearms on the table, providing ventilation to her injured hand. "So ask. What do you want to know?"

"How could David be mine if I took precautions?"

"You didn't."

"How the hell do you know?" he demanded, frowning sternly. "Or was that a game? Chesty Sharon got to make it while little sister got to watch?"

Marnie grabbed her purse and scooted to the edge of the booth. He caught her arm. "I'm sorry. Uncalled for. Please." She worked her arm free, but his eyes arrested her. "Please, Marnie."

Perhaps it was hearing her name coming from his lips for the first time in seventeen years, or perhaps it was her own need to set the record straight after so long a time. For whatever reason, she slid back into the booth.

"I can see why you might not hold Sharon in high regard," she told him stiffly. "After all, she was easy. But I don't deserve your insults."

"I said I was sorry and I meant it. Okay?" She conceded with a terse nod. "So how do you know what happened?"

"Sharon told me that you didn't have . . . that you were . . . unprepared one night. According to her, things had gotten pretty, uh, hot." She glanced up at him inquiringly.

"I'm with you so far. Go on."

"She didn't want you to stop, so she lied to you. She told you that she was taking birth control pills."

He gazed into near space a moment, then shook his head. "I don't remember."

"You'd been drinking beer all afternoon."

"Then it's possible, I guess."

"Colonel Kincaid, I—"

"Will you please call me Law?" he said irritably. "I remember wrestling with you in the sand and rubbing suntan oil on your back. So call me Law, okay?"

He remembered. At least a little bit. She derived tremendous pleasure in knowing that. His memories of her might be dim, but they were there.

"It doesn't matter if David is or isn't your son," she said quietly. "Our lives will go on exactly as before."

"You're forgetting one important point, Marnie."

"What?"

"The letters."

She raised her hands helplessly. "How many times do I have to tell you that I didn't write them?"

"That makes them even more of a problem."

"I don't see—"

"If you didn't write them, someone else did."

Thinking of it from that angle caused her brow to furrow with concern. "I'm beginning to see your point."

"You say you don't want anything from me."

"I don't."

"But whoever is writing the letters does. And that makes David as vulnerable as I am."

"You don't think someone would hurt him, do you?"

"I don't know. Probably not. But that's a possibility."

She pulled her lower lip through her teeth. "What are we going to do?"

"I didn't mean to worry you. It's just something for you to be aware of while we try to figure out whose game this is. Any ideas?"

"None. David looks like you, but you'd almost have to be standing side by side for anyone to realize it."

"What about the doctor who delivered him? Would he have a motive for blackmailing me?"

"I don't know. We moved away from that neighborhood and I haven't heard of him in years. Besides, he didn't know who had fathered Sharon's baby."

"Could she have confided in a close friend?"

"I don't think so, but anything's possible. You think that somebody knew and, once you got famous, they remembered and decided to cash in?"

"That's my theory, yeah." He studied his coffee for a moment, cleared his throat, then in an off-handed manner said, "That rest home where your mother's living is certainly deluxe."

"It's operated by the church Dad was affiliated with. They give a price break to minister's widows . . . so you can stop right there thinking what you're thinking." Quickly he raised his head. Marnie was glaring dangerously at him.

"It hasn't always been easy," she said in an angry undertone, "but I've done all right for myself and David. We're not rich by any means. He hasn't had everything he's ever wanted, and for that reason he appreciates material things more than other kids his age. But we're not destitute. He's never gone without food, shelter, or clothing and, most important, love."

"I just——"

"Be quiet and listen to me," she commanded, surprising both of them with her ferocity. "I love David. He loves me. All you've thought about so far is how this might affect *you* if it gets out. If it's possible, with your colossal ego in the way, think about how it could affect David.

"He's at an impressionable, sensitive stage. He's a wonderful kid. I don't want anything to happen that will upset his wholesome outlook on life.

"And that goes for finding out that his father is a hotshot astronaut who sleeps with a woman only if *he's* protected and who drives like a maniac. If you do or say anything that even hints at harming him, you'll wish you were still in orbit, Colonel Kincaid." She drew in a sharp breath. "Now, will you please take me home?"

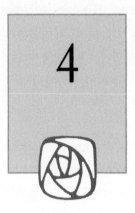

4

There were two individuals waiting for Law when he returned home. Both were female. Both were blond. Both were brown-eyed. One had two legs, the other four. One was angry. One was jubilant.

The four-legged blonde, a Labrador retriever named Venus, bounded across the lawn that was kept immaculate by a professional crew Law never saw. They came while he was at work, did the job, and left an invoice in the mailbox. A housekeeper maintained the interior of the house using the same method. His domicile wasn't typical bachelor digs.

Venus nearly knocked him over when she jumped up on her rear legs and began to lick his collarbone because that's as far as she could reach.

"Hey, girl," he said, pushing her down affectionately. Bending over, he picked up the evening newspaper and scratched the dog behind the ears. He sailed the rolled-up newspaper across the yard. Obediently Venus loped after it, tongue dangling from the corner of her mouth.

He doubted he could appease the other blonde by scratching her behind the ears and throwing a newspaper for her to fetch. Not for the first time, he wished that all the females in his life were as uncomplicated and easy to get along with as Venus.

"Hi," he said, flashing his most winning smile.

"You're only an hour late," she reported peevishly. "That damned dog nearly ate me alive when I went indoors."

"She's jealous of other women."

He took his mail out of the box and sorted through it. Only one letter caught his eye. The plain white envelope had been addressed in what had become a familiar script. He slid it into his breast pocket and dropped the rest of the mail on the lacquered hall table as he went through the door.

"Is that all you can say?" Venus bounded in carrying the newspaper. The other blonde pointed at her accusingly. "It nearly shredded my stockings when it took swipes at my legs."

"She was protecting my house against an intruder."

"Intruder? You gave me a door key, the combination of your alarm system, and told me to let myself in."

"I did? When?"

"When you made the date for tonight."

"We have a date?"

She was fifteen years his junior, had a so-so face, legs that started in her armpits, and a tanned cleavage that would normally have caused him to salivate with lust. Having her in bed would make him the envy of every guy he knew.

But it had been a lousy day. Pacifying an aggravated blond bimbo was going to require more energy than he was willing to expend.

"You didn't remember that we had a date?" she whined petulantly.

"No."

"We met last week at a party. Lots of astronauts were there."

He didn't remember which party. After so many they began to blur together, like the bimbos. In fact, he didn't remember much of what had happened to him before Marnie had looked up at him with serious, misty eyes and confirmed that, yes, the strapping lad with Law Kincaid's bone structure and Law Kincaid's coloring was Law Kincaid's son.

"Look, uh . . . ?"

"Suzette."

"Suzette, I'm sorry," he said, running a hand through his hair. "I, uh, something came up today at the center and I couldn't get away. We had to do this antigravity thing, see, and I'm bone tired. Let's do this some other night, okay?"

She didn't buy his ingratiating smile or untruthful excuse. "Say, is this a brush-off?"

He studied her sulky red mouth and accusing eyes for a moment, then said, "Say, yeah, it is. Where's my key?"

She commissioned him to do something that was an anatomical impossibility and ground the latchkey into his hand, almost breaking the skin of his palm with the jagged teeth.

Venus growled and nipped at Suzette's tapping high heels all the way to the front door. After it was slammed behind her, the dog looked back at him with a complacent expression.

"You jealous bitch. Want a Flavor Snack?"

Venus followed him through the house that a homosexual couple had lived in and decorated before they split up and sold the creative result of their liaison to Law.

He liked the clean modern lines and spacious, uncluttered rooms. Absently he fed the colorful tropical fish in the aquarium that was mounted in the wall dividing the dining room and kitchen.

Taking the envelope from his pocket, he read his latest letter. The threats of exposure were more vitriolic than before. He reread the paragraphs several times and became so steeped in the puzzle of who could have sent them that Venus had to lick his hand to remind him of the promised treat.

He got her a dog biscuit, himself a beer, and slid open the glass door that opened onto the redwood deck. There he shed his clothes and, naked, slid into the hot tub that comprised one end of the Italian tile swimming pool, which was the envy of even his most affluent friends.

He lived on a military salary, modest when compared to most young executives. But he had no one to spend money on except himself. He lived well and was willing to splurge extravagantly on creature comforts.

He'd already forgotten the blonde. He couldn't have picked her out of a lineup. His thoughts centered on the boy he had met that afternoon.

"Damn good-looking kid," he told Venus, who was so pleased to be included in his private reverie that she braved dunking her muzzle into the bubbling hot water to lick his shoulder.

Any man would be proud to have a son like David Hibbs . . . David Kincaid.

He'd been reared right. He treated his mother with respect. Even though he'd been ecstatic over getting to drive the Porsche, he'd remembered to say thank you afterward. He'd buckled his seat belt without being told to. He drove conscientiously and well.

Law could find little fault with the way Marnie had raised his son.

His son?

Was he ready to admit it?

Until today that summer had been a pleasant but vague memory. What did he really know about Marnie Hibbs and her family? She could be just a damn clever con who assumed that brave-little-soldier demeanor when it served her purpose. She could be just a damn good actress who convincingly pretended to be offended when accused of sending folks threatening letters through the mail.

She certainly stood to gain a lot if he did acknowledge David as his son. Rearing a kid nowadays was expensive. As the only bachelor currently in the astronaut office, he listened to his cohorts lamenting daily on the high cost of teenagers.

Freelancing as an illustrator might be lucrative at times, but it wasn't constant or reliable income. There could be months between sizable commissions. Maybe this Hibbs broad was in an economic slump because of her mother's medical bills and had devised this nefarious plan as a means of getting some quick cash.

But she sure as hell had put him in his place when he'd subtly suggested that money was her motive. She was a tiny package of woman, but when riled she was as hot as a stick of dynamite. And damned exciting.

Swearing, Law left the hot tub and padded back into the kitchen for another beer. As he sipped it, Venus sitting worshipfully at his dripping feet, he thought about all the ramifications a teenage son would have on his life. The blond bimbos would have to taper off considerably. And when he got assigned to another shuttle mission, who would—

"This is nuts!" he exclaimed to the empty house. "The kid's probably not even mine."

But as he headed for his shower in the master bathroom,

he smiled when he recalled how loud and rambunctious and thoroughly delightful David was, and frowned when he recalled kissing the lady David called Mom—frowned because that kiss had been short but explosive. That kiss had nearly blown the top of his head off. That kiss was one reason the blond bimbo hadn't looked at all appealing tonight.

"G'night, Mom." David stood framed in the doorway. There was a single light burning over Marnie's drawing board where she was doodling, trying to come up with an idea for a jewelry store ad.

"Going to bed so early?"

"Coach ran our asses off this afternoon. I'm tired."

She didn't scold his language. Tonight she chose to ignore it because she knew he was using it to test her reaction. Sometimes no reaction was the best one.

"Sleep well. Remember you're supposed to mow the lawn tomorrow."

"Five bucks?"

"Seven if you edge and sweep up too."

"Deal." He didn't leave. He picked at the wood in the doorframe, a sign that he was about to broach a sensitive subject. "What was Law Kincaid really doing here today?"

She fumbled her pencil. It rolled to the floor. "Doing here?" she repeated feebly. "You know why he was here."

"How come you didn't tell me you had called him? I mean, it seems like you would have mentioned it."

"Well, I didn't actually call him. I, uh, called NASA and asked if I could use his face in my drawings. I guess they wanted to check me out before granting permission and sent him personally. I was as surprised as you when he showed up here."

She'd never lied to David in his life . . . unless one counted the hundreds of times he'd asked who his father was. Those had been lies of omission, kind lies meant to protect, not absolute fabrications like the whopper she'd just told.

"Oh. Well, it was great meeting him. Did you think he was cool?" he asked eagerly.

"Very cool."

"I thought he might be stuck-up, but he was just like a real person."

"He *is* a real person."

"Yeah, but you know what I mean."

"Yes, I know."

"Do you think he'll remember me, that he'll ever come back?"

Marnie went to him and smoothed back the hair that had fallen over his brow, having to stretch her arm up to reach it. She hated reminders like that of how much he'd grown. The time had gone by so fast. So fast.

"I doubt we'll ever see him again, David," she said kindly.

Her thoughts filtered back to that hostile drive from the coffee shop to her house, during which nothing had been said. She'd bade Law a curt good-bye at the curb. He hadn't tarried but had angrily peeled out, furious over the dressing-down she'd given him. She didn't regret a single word of it. He'd deserved it for intimating that she was a liar and blackmailer.

"I wouldn't count on ever seeing him again. He's awfully busy and meets a lot of people."

"I know," David said, "but I think he liked me. Wouldn't it be cool if we could, you know, be friends with him?"

Her throat swelled almost shut, but she forced a smile and gave him a long hug. "You'd better get to bed. You need the rest. The big game is only a few days away."

"Noooo problem." As he normally did whenever he exited a room, he jumped up to swat the ceiling, then dashed out.

Marnie listened to his footsteps thudding on the hollow stairs of the old house as he took them two at a time. Instead of smiling fondly as she usually did, she blotted tears from her eyes.

Letters. Anonymous letters. From the day Sharon had told her that she was pregnant with Law Kincaid's baby, Marnie had fantasized about how the child might draw him back into her life. In her fantasies it was always for some catastrophic reason like David needing a kidney transplant, or a blood transfusion, never anything as innocuous as a letter.

But Law had entered her life again. And he was larger than life, more heart-stoppingly handsome. The azure blue of his eyes hadn't dimmed, but if anything had become more vivid. His confident smile, the loose-limbed, cocky gait of a jet fighter pilot, the way sunlight shone on his hair, had all been achingly familiar because those images had been locked inside Marnie's heart for seventeen years.

Those images hadn't been dulled by the grief she had suffered since: the loss of her sister and father, and her mother's declining health. Those images of Law had sustained her through her struggle to get a college degree, work at a job, and take care of David all at the same time. Those images had spelled doom for any love relationships with real potential.

The only man she had ever loved now held sway over her life again. For the second time her future rested in his hands. Only now he was aware of it.

She was partially to blame for the anxiety she was experiencing. She could have laughed off the letters' allegations, categorically denied them, and told Law that someone was playing a practical joke on him, no doubt a freeloader who had seen David and noticed the resemblance.

But Marnie's moral code wouldn't have allowed her to take the easy way out. When asked, her conscience had given her no alternative but to tell Law the truth.

Unfortunately how Law responded to that truth could seriously change their lives. If David woke up to the realization that Law was the father he'd always been curious about, and Law spurned him, how would David withstand the rejection?

Or if Law decided to acknowledge his son, how could she cope with living without David? He had been the only fine, positive element in her life. Law had given him to her. Law could now take him away.

Marnie looked down at the hand she'd spilled coffee on. The redness was fading, but there were still traces of butter shining on her skin. Closing her eyes, she recalled the feel of his fingertips gently stroking her hand. Involuntarily she groaned.

She loved Law Kincaid with an unrequited passion that made her ache. She loved his son with equal intensity. Law had never been hers. And as of today, she was at risk of losing David.

5

Diet soda, please."

"Make that two."

At the sound of his voice, Marnie spun around. "What are you doing here?"

"Buying soda," he said with a careless smile. "And give us a bag of that popcorn too, please."

The man operating the concession stand got their drinks and the popcorn without ever really taking his eyes off Law. "Don't I know you?"

Law broke into a big smile. "You might."

The man studied his face as he counted back Law's change from a ten-dollar bill. Marnie had tried to pay for her own drink, but over the counter their hands had engaged in a silent slapping battle that she eventually lost.

"Oh, hell, yeah," the man said with a guffaw. "You work at Wal-Mart, right? Sporting goods department?"

Law's smile faltered, but only marginally. "Right. Which team are you rooting for?"

"The Tornadoes."

"You're my man. Thanks." Law then elbowed Marnie out of line and toward one of the concrete ramps leading into the high school stadium.

She held in her laughter as long as she could.

"Shut up," Law growled out of the side of his mouth. "That happens just often enough to keep me humble."

He didn't look humble. He gave every appearance of a man who had the world by the tail. He was wearing white shorts, a navy-blue polo shirt that fit his trim torso like a glove, a NASA dozer cap, and the aviator sunglasses that attracted attention rather than repelled it. Walking beside him, Marnie saw heads turn whether in recognition or plain admiration.

"Thank you for the drink."

"Don't mention it. Want some popcorn?"

"No thanks."

Since both his hands were occupied, he used his tongue to scoop a bite from the top of the box. "I got another letter," he said casually as he munched.

"You did?"

"Hmm. The same day I came to see you. Which way?"

"Down there where all the blue and black is." She nodded toward a section of the stadium where there was so much spectator enthusiasm going on, it looked like a wild animal feeding frenzy.

He moved aside so she could precede him down the steep concrete steps. "What did the letter say?" she asked over her shoulder.

"More of the same. We'll talk about it later. After the game."

"I thought since you didn't call or come by the next day that—"

"That you'd seen the last of me?"

"Yes," she replied with candor.

"Were you glad or sad about that?"

"I'm not sure."

Her feelings had been ambiguous when first one day, then another passed without his making any further contact. On the one hand, she had been vastly relieved. On the other, she couldn't bear the thought of never seeing him again.

Then, too, there had been David's disappointment to contend with when his idol failed to follow up an initial meeting with a telephone call.

"How about here?" he asked, nudging her into a row of seats.

"Fine."

Marnie waved at David's teammates' parents, nearly all of whom had stopped cheering in order to stare curiously at Law and her. She'd never attended any school sporting event with a date before. There had been well-meaning attempts at matchmaking with the single soccer coach the spring before. Marnie had demurred.

This season he'd had a girlfriend who cheered the team

from the stands, so Marnie had been spared the embarrassment of contrivances designed to force them into each other's company.

She'd never confided to any of the matchmakers that the coach had called her on two separate occasions asking for a date. Both times she'd made such lame excuses that he'd apparently gotten discouraged and given up.

Now she felt as visible as a lightning bug in a Mason jar as Law lowered himself close beside her on the bleacher. They had the attention of everybody seated within ten rows of them.

"Heard anything about the telephone book commission?" Law asked.

"Not yet. I still have my fingers crossed." She held up her hand, the middle finger overlapping the index one. He caught it by the wrist and tipped up his sunglasses to examine it.

"How's the burn?"

"The skin never even blistered. The butter worked, I guess."

"Good." He held her hand for another second or two before letting it go. "You look like the team mascot," he commented as he tossed back a fistful of popcorn. "You should be down on the field leading cheers."

She was wearing black shorts and a blue and black striped jersey with "David's Mom" embroidered over her left breast. "All the mothers dress in the team jersey."

"None of them look like you, though."

She couldn't see his eyes through his glasses, but she knew they were moving over her. It made her uncomfortably warm. She turned her head toward the field. "There's David."

"What number is—oh, there he is."

David and his teammates were jogging toward the sidelines after undergoing a brisk pre-game warm-up on the field. When he spotted them sitting together in the stands, Marnie saw lights go on behind his blue eyes, even from that distance. His smile deepened and he waved enthusiastically. Law waved back and gave him the thumbs-up sign.

"His team is going to win," he remarked.

"How do you know?"

"The kid's a winner. It's written all over him."

By the end of the first half Marnie was afraid Law's prediction would prove wrong. The Tornadoes were behind one to nothing. It had been a frustrating half for both teams, each coming close to scoring many times, the attempts being thwarted by talented goalies. The mood in the stands had reached a hysterical pitch. Emotions were running high.

So when their bare thighs happened to brush against each other, Marnie jerked hers away from Law's. Each of the hairs on his leg seemed to conduct an electric current.

"Excuse me," she said breathlessly.

"Nothing to excuse." Subconsciously she was running her hand up and down her thigh where his had touched. Noting that, he added, "Relax. I don't have anything you can catch by casual contact."

She stopped rubbing her leg and frowned at him, perturbed. "Do you enjoy that?"

"What? Casual contact?"

"Placing women in awkward positions."

"Actually awkward positions have never been a big turn-on for me. I like to keep sex as uncomplicated as possible and concentrate on the basics."

Wanting to wipe away his twitching smile, she reverted to the serious subject that had brought them together. "What did it say? The letter."

The sun had sunk behind the other side of the stadium, causing a giant shadow to fall over the bleachers where they were sitting. Law had removed his sunglasses. She watched his amused eyes turn somber.

"More of the same."

"More threatening?" she asked, concerned for David's safety.

"Not exactly. I was reminded of the field day the media would have if David's story were leaked. Not that I needed to be reminded," he said beneath his breath.

"That would be no picnic for David either."

"I know that," he said defensively. "I'm not the selfish bastard you obviously take me for. Right now I have to think logically and pragmatically, not emotionally. The only way we're going to catch this guy is to start reasoning like him. Okay?"

She nodded. He seemed momentarily mollified. "I make a big target to throw mud at. Whoever is writing the letters is intelligent enough to realize that and use it as leverage. He's no crackpot. This has been a well-thought-out plan to destroy my career."

"I can see how it might make life uncomfortable, but how could the disclosure of a youthful indiscretion destroy your career?"

"NASA has regained some of the credibility it lost after the *Challenger* accident."

"Thanks mainly to you."

He gave a self-effacing shrug. "But the administrators are still as jumpy as cats. They don't want anything to go wrong. They certainly don't want any scandal. And if a picture of the illegitimate son I've never acknowledged showed up on the covers of the tabloids, what do you think my chances would be for getting another mission?"

"And you want another?"

His expression implied that was the dumbest question he'd ever heard. "Damn right. There are a limited number of missions with a limited number of crewmen for each one. I want to fly as many as I possibly can before I get too old or before a glitch shows up on a routine EKG or before some younger pilot retires me. Oh, yeah, I want to go again."

"You love it, don't you, Law?"

"It's right up there with prime rib, Ray Charles, and sex."

"I don't think I understood until now just how vulnerable you are. It never occurred to me that public exposure of this might affect your career."

"The center wouldn't fire me. But bad PR would make

me dead meat around the astronaut office. I'd be training other guys to do what I'm dying to do myself." His lips narrowed. "Whoever is threatening me knows how important space exploration is to me."

"It's not me," she said earnestly, reflexively pressing her hand to her chest. "It would be much better for David, and for me, if things stayed exactly as they are. Knowing that you're his father would only complicate his life."

That sparked his temper. "Why?"

"Because you're you, that's why. What would you do with a teenage son?"

"Go to more soccer games."

"And fewer parties."

"I see you've been keeping up with me."

She fell silent. It wouldn't do for him to know that the first thing she looked for in every morning's newspaper was a mention of him in any context. As often as not a picture of him could be found in the society pages.

"There's the whistle," she said, drawing their attention back to the field.

The Tornadoes scored a point less than two minutes into the half, tying the score. But tension mounted as the minutes of the second half dwindled until only one remained on the clock. It seemed that the game would go into overtime. Everyone in the stadium was on his feet and hoarse from yelling encouragement to the players whose spirits and energy levels were beginning to flag.

"Here, stand up here where you can see better," Law

told Marnie. His hands spanned her waist and lifted her to stand on the bench in front of them. "Better?"

"Much." For the first time since the game began, she had an unobstructed view of the field.

"Oh, no!" Marnie, along with everyone else in the stands, groaned as a Tornado's attempt at a goal missed by inches. "Get control of the ball, David! Get it from . . . that's it!" she hollered, cupping her hands around her mouth. She jumped up and down, stamping on the bench. To secure her, Law placed his hands on either side of her waist.

"Careful there, don't fall." Then he cursed as an opposing player stole the ball from David, who had been skillfully maneuvering it toward the goal. "Get it back, David! Stay on him, stay—"

"Go, David, go!" Marnie screamed as David deftly stole the ball from right between the other player's feet without fouling him.

"Twenty seconds!" she shouted. "Fifteen, David! Help him out, guys! Block that kid! Lord, he's been doing that to them all afternoon and they— That's a foul, ref!" she shouted, aiming an accusing finger. "Where are your glasses? Ten seconds. Oh, damn. David, do something! Five sec—"

Her last words were drowned out by the roar that went up when David fired a shot past the goalie to score the winning point. Pandemonium broke out on the field, on the sidelines, in the stands. The fans went wild.

Cheering louder than any were Marnie and Law. Caught

up in the madness of the moment, she whirled around and landed in his arms. Lifting her off her feet, he hugged her tightly and made crazy spirals between the bleachers.

"I can't believe it. I can't believe it," she chanted, laughing and crying all at once. She smiled down into Law's face. He smiled up into hers.

Then their smiles dissolved and left them looking at each other quizzically. Their eyes connected with a different emotion, but one just as potent as exultation.

Simultaneously they realized that one of his hands was supporting her derriere and the other was splayed over her back. Her arms were wound around his neck. Her knees had caught him at crotch level and her breasts were even with his mouth.

Gradually he lowered her, until their positions were reversed and she was gazing up at him with wide, uncomprehending eyes. She slowly removed her arms from around his neck, but her hands came to rest on the broad upper half of his chest.

The impact on her senses was so stunning that for several moments all she could do was stare up at him. He seemed just as surprised as she, but he recovered his equanimity first.

"Your kid's a hell of a shooter."

"Thank you," she replied huskily. Suddenly aware that she was still touching him, she dropped her hands to her sides. Law released her, though she could still feel the warm imprint of his hand on her bottom.

"Want to join that melee?"

The clock had run out. On the field the players were engaged in a victory rite. Each had a canned drink, which he shook hard before opening, then aimed the spray at his fellow players.

"I wouldn't miss it," she said, and laughed.

Together they jogged down the stadium steps, climbed over the railing, and ran out on the field. David met them. Exuberantly he swept Marnie into a huge, sweaty embrace and swung her around, much as Law had done only moments earlier.

"You were wonderful, David, wonderful." She pounded him on the back and gave him a kiss that he was too excited to be embarrassed by.

"Nice going," Law said in an understatement, giving David a sound wallop between the shoulder blades. Then the two of them shook hands.

"Thanks for coming, Colonel Kincaid."

"The guy who scores the winning point gets to call me Law."

David grinned, abashed. "Law, we're all going out for pizza. The whole team. Everybody's invited. Can you come?"

"I'd love to."

David executed a back handspring and let out a Comanche yell. "Okay, meet you back here. We gotta get the trophy."

Since he was the captain, he and the coach formally

accepted the trophy from the officials in the center of the field. Standing close to Marnie, Law slid his arm across her shoulders and gave her neck a quick squeeze when David stepped forward to make the acceptance speech.

"I'd like to thank the school board and faculty who supported us through this season. Student body, you've all been great!" An enormous roar went up from the stands. He waited for it to die down. "I'd like to thank Coach. We couldn't have done it without him." Another cheer of approval went up from parents and players alike. "I accept this trophy on behalf of every member of the team. Go, Tornadoes!" he shouted.

Law bent down and placed his mouth close to Marnie's ear. "He's eloquent too."

"Thank you."

Luckily the victory celebration going on around them kept him from seeing her tears. Bearing the weight of his arm on her shoulders in addition to the love in her heart for him and his son, she had almost crumpled.

While gravitating toward the parking lot, the three of them engaged in a heated debate over transportation to the pizza parlor. Marnie was defeated two to one. "Just like the game score," she said, conceding.

"Don't be a sore loser." Law was supremely pleased with the outcome of the vote and made no attempt to hide it.

She and David were led to a sporty four-wheel-drive vehicle. "How many sets of wheels have you got?" David shouted from the backseat of the convertible Land Rover once they were buckled in and under way.

"Only this and the Porsche."

"I'm sorry all the guys ganged up on you back there. They really lost their cool. They don't know how to act around somebody famous." He feigned a sophisticated annoyance that brought smiles to the lips of the adults. "Nobody could believe you came just to watch me play."

"I didn't mind signing a few autographs."

"They're usually clustered around Mom."

"They are not!" Marnie protested.

"Oh, yeah?" Law asked.

"You ought to hear 'em talking about her," David continued. "They're all in love, or rather in lust, with her."

"David Hibbs, will you kindly refrain from—"

"You know they are, Mom." He addressed Law's face in the rearview mirror. "See, she's not as old as most of my friends' moms. And she's a lot better-looking. She's not all uptight and cranky either, but really cool."

"Really?" Law commented dryly.

"Yeah, no foolin'." David pulled a frown. "I'm glad they like her, but one guy started shooting off his mouth and saying that he'd like to, uh, you know, get her naked and take her to bed. I had to punch him out."

"David!" Horrified, Marnie turned in her seat to gape at him. "You never told me that."

"Don't worry. He's scum, not one of my close friends."

To Law's reflection he said, "Most of the time it's okay the way my friends carry on about her. They tease me about her being available." He chuckled. "I even had a senior ask me if it was okay if he invited her to the prom. I think he was only joking." He looked at Marnie. "He didn't really ask you, did he?"

"Certainly not."

He shrugged and addressed Law in the mirror again. "I guess it's okay if they flirt with her since she's not my real mom. She's really my aunt. My real mom died when I was four."

"What about your dad?"

Marnie swiveled in her seat again, this time to face Law. She glared a silent warning at him.

David, however, answered the question with aplomb. It was one he'd had to answer every time he made a new acquaintance. "I never knew who my dad was, but Mom said it didn't matter because I'm an individual and that where you're going is more important than where you come from." He pointed between their shoulders. "Up there, Law. On the right."

The din inside the restaurant was deafening. The harried manager paled when the rowdy Tornadoes stormed through, claiming tables. Orders were taken and sodas were dispensed as rapidly as possible. The team sat at one long table in the middle of the dining area while parents and fans in general, among them several groups of giggling girls, sat at surrounding tables.

Law and Marnie occupied one on the periphery. It gave them a modicum of privacy. "I guess I should feel honored."

Marnie blotted her mouth on the paper napkin and pushed her empty plate aside. "Why, for getting invited to this victory celebration?"

"That and for getting to sit with the most popular girl."

"David exaggerates."

"I don't think so. I've been on the receiving end of some envious stares all night. What's with you and the coach?"

"Nothing. He's got a girlfriend."

"I don't think she was his first choice, though." Marnie gave Law a reproving glance. Not put off by it, he leaned across the table and studied her in the wavering candle-light. "It's reassuring to know that the younger generation has good taste."

"Thanks. But that doesn't get you off the hook for baiting David on the way here. If you want information, ask me."

"Okay. How many have there been?"

"How many what?"

"Men."

"None of your business."

"No husband?"

"No."

"How come?"

"What possible interest could that be to you? I wouldn't dare ask how many women there've been in your life since I met you in Galveston."

"Too many to count."

"Precisely."

"But that's not the case with you, is it? I'll bet the number of men who've made it to your bed could be counted on one hand."

That stung her ego. "Why do you say that?"

"Because having David around would cramp a romantic relationship. Am I right?"

"You couldn't be more wrong," she said in the same steely voice with which she'd told him off several nights earlier. "A romantic relationship might cramp my life with David. Rest assured, Colonel Kincaid, that your son has been reared in a moral climate."

"I haven't conceded yet that he's my son."

"Oh," she said, taken aback. "I assumed that since you came to the game, made an effort to see David again, that you were positive."

"Before I proceed—"

"Proceed?" she asked, panicked. "Proceed to do what?"

"I don't even know yet. First I've got to be certain I fathered him. You can understand that, can't you?"

"You've got nothing to go on except my word for it and his remarkable resemblance to you."

"I understand there's a blood test," Law said slowly. "It can't prove paternity, but it can be decisive in eliminating some possibilities."

"I've heard of it."

"I want David and me to have it. I want to eliminate any doubt."

"You feel that's necessary?"

"Yes, Marnie. I do. For my own peace of mind."

Marnie sighed and said, "I can't very well stop you, can I?"

"Will you cooperate?"

She thought a moment before answering. "David had to have a physical before the soccer season began. They took blood then. His records will be on file."

"I'll handle it. Who do I contact?"

She wrote down the name of the clinic where David had recently had a sports physical and handed the slip of paper to Law just as David joined them.

He dropped to his knees beside their table and began to beat on it like a bongo drum. "I'm ready to leave whenever you are. I've wiped out everybody on the video games. They've banished me because they all owe me money."

Law laughed indulgently and helped Marnie from her chair. She tried unsuccessfully to divide their tab; Law sternly refused. They left under a hail of cheers for the team captain who had saved the day for the Tornadoes, and they cheered his heroic guest.

Within minutes they were on the freeway. "Hey, Law, you missed the turnoff to the stadium," David pointed out from the backseat.

"But not the turnoff to my house."

6

Your house?" Marnie asked.

"I thought you might like to take a swim and cool off."

"You mean it, Law? You've got a pool? Mom, he's got a pool."

"It's getting late."

"It's not a school night. Please?"

Since Law had control of the car, the choice wasn't left to her, but she was unenthusiastic over the idea of going to his house. She didn't want David getting too chummy with the celebrity who had waltzed into his life and who would in all probability waltz right out again when the novelty of having a son wore off.

And if Law's sense of responsibility made him feel obligated to claim David, how could her old house, which desperately needed new plumbing, possibly compete with a gorgeous modern home with a swimming pool in the backyard and an aquarium in the dining room wall?

The aquarium was just one of the thousand things David labeled *"Cool!"* as he moved from one room to another. The golden Labrador snarled at Marnie but took to David instantly and trotted along beside him, wagging her tail and licking his knees.

"Is this a totally awesome house or what?" he exclaimed when he stepped out onto the deck to admire the landscaped pool area.

"Dive in," Law told him. "But take the cleats off first, please."

David hastily stripped to his briefs and dove in without a second's hesitation. "Good form," Law observed.

"Ten summers of lessons at the Y," Marnie said.

"Does he excel at everything he tries?"

"Yes." She gave Law a sidelong glance. "And he didn't get that overachiever's drive from his mother."

They watched as David lapped the pool several times before stopping to rest. Venus stayed even with him, racing up and down the deck, barking excitedly. When he came up for air, she licked his face.

"The dog loves me." Laughing, he dodged her fervent affection.

"She hasn't been exercised today. Why don't you take her for a walk?" Law suggested. "A red Ferrari lives two blocks down to the south. It's usually parked out front this time of night."

David heaved himself out of the pool and accepted a towel and Venus's leash from Law, who was holding both out to him. "Come on, girl. Be back in a minute, folks."

The boy and his newly devoted companion went through the privacy fence gate. It slapped closed behind them. "I think Venus would run off with him tonight if he asked her," Law remarked. "The unfaithful hussy."

"He's always wanted a dog."

"Why hasn't he ever had one?" His brows met in a frown above the bridge of his nose.

"Mother. Pets make her nervous. I haven't had time to look into getting one since she went to the nursing home."

Law pondered that a minute, then nodded toward a cabana on the far side of the pool. "The little girls' changing room is through there. You'll find an assortment of suits in the closet, but I'm not sure I'll have anything small enough to fit you."

"I don't want a suit."

He took a step closer. His voice deepened. His grin turned suggestive. "That's an even better idea."

"I didn't mean that."

"You've been skinny-dipping before. I remember."

"You remember wrong if you're referring to the night you and Sharon swam naked in the Gulf."

"Ah, that's right. You wouldn't take off your suit. Both of us tried to get you to go along, but you wouldn't."

"You could have been charged with corrupting the morals of a minor."

"You didn't give me a chance to corrupt yours. You started crying and ran home. Why?"

She shook her head dumbly, mesmerized by the way the moonlight turned the top of his head silver. It looked exactly as it had that night on the Galveston beach when Sharon had called her a chicken and threatened her with strangulation if she told their parents what she was up to.

Law, a smidgen more tolerant, had wheedled, "Come on, squirt. It won't hurt. Lightning's not going to strike you."

She had desperately wanted to join him in the warm salt water but was too self-conscious of her juvenile body and too afraid of getting caught.

"Why didn't you skinny-dip with me that night? Were you afraid of me?"

"No," she exclaimed on a whisper.

"Why'd you cry, Marnie? Were you embarrassed?"

"I cried because I was mad."

"Mad? At me?"

"At you. At Sharon. I hated you for being able to treat it so casually when I couldn't. Mostly I was mad at myself. I wanted to join in so much, you see, but lacked the courage."

The pupils of his eyes contracted a fraction. "Now's your chance to make up for that missed opportunity."

"I still lack the courage."

"I don't." He worked off his athletic shoes and peeled off his socks. The polo shirt was whipped over his head in one fluid motion. It brushed her bare legs on its way down to the deck.

"Law?"

"Hmm?" He unsnapped his shorts.

Marnie's eyes hungrily roved over his chest. The triangle of blond fuzz that had been growing in its center when he was twenty-two had thickened and fanned out to cover it all. The color had ripened to a golden brown. It swirled and whorled over the hard, curved muscles and around his nipples, giving credence to the brainstorm of an entrepreneur who had recently proposed to market a Law Kincaid beefcake poster.

His idea was to have a bare-chested Law wearing a mock space suit opened down the front to his navel. He would pose Law in front of a rocket, a none-too-subtle symbol. It would sell millions, he had promised. There wouldn't be a need for tax dollars to finance future NASA space probes. The coffers would be full of money from the pocketbooks of slavering women.

NASA had been horrified, of course. They hadn't honored the preposterous idea with an official comment. The media had had fun with the story for several days before it died a natural death.

But now Marnie, dry-mouthed, damp-palmed, and weak-kneed, thought the guy's idea had merit.

Law dropped his running shorts and kicked them aside,

then hooked his thumbs into the elastic waistband of his underwear. Instinctively Marnie extended her hand to deter his. When she made contact with warm skin, she snatched it back.

"I cannot let David find me swimming naked in your pool, Law," she said. "This is a ridiculous, childish game. Stop it."

"Then stop being such a spoilsport and go get into a suit."

Blue eyes challenged gray. Gray might have held out longer if blue hadn't raised his brows inquiringly and hooked his thumbs back into his briefs. Blue won.

Marnie turned and marched stiffly to the door of the cabana and soundly closed it behind her. Three swimsuits and ten minutes later she emerged wearing a black maillot. The material was stretchy enough to conform to her slight figure, even though the suit was a size too large.

Confidently she walked to the board, bounced up and down to test its spring, then executed a fine dive. When she surfaced, he was applauding as he floated on his back toward the side of the pool, kicking his feet to keep himself afloat.

"Very good."

"Thanks."

She swam toward the ladder and was halfway up it when his hand closed around her ankle. Tugging on it, he pulled her back into the water and pressed her backward against the tile wall.

When his legs drifted against hers, she sucked in a sharp breath. "Law, you're—"

"Um-huh. I like swimming naked. It feels good."

"And that's the creed you abide by, isn't it? If it feels good, do it."

"And your creed is if it feels good, it must be sinful." He sipped a drop of water off her earlobe and glanced her neck with his lips. "For once, Miss Goody-Two-Shoes, why don't you just relax and go with the flow? Take a chance. Do something daring, something—"

She gave both his shoulders a shove that pushed him away and created a huge splash. "That's why you're doing this, isn't it?" she demanded angrily. "Because it's exciting, challenging, *daring*. Having a teenage boy walk in on his mother and a naked man in a swimming pool must be a thrill you haven't experienced yet."

She reached for the guardrail of the ladder and once again was almost up before he hauled her back into the water, but not as gently as before.

This time his hands slipped into the notches of her armpits. The heels of his palms pressed against the sides of her breasts, making them swell above the top of her suit. He noticed. And noticed, too, the enticing thrust of her nipples against the wet fabric plastered to them. He held her close enough to ensure that she felt him, hard and ready against her middle.

"The only reason I'm doing this," he said through clenched teeth, "is because I got my hands on you once today. All I've thought about since then is getting them on you again."

He lowered his eyes to her lips. They were wet with swimming pool water and the nervous, reflexive action of her own tongue. Her lipstick had worn off. Marnie couldn't know how sexy that looked to him.

"If I'd had as much sense seventeen years ago as I do now," he added on a growl, "I'd have ripped off your suit and dragged you into the surf with me that night on the beach. Maybe if I had helped you to overcome your inhibitions, if I'd acquainted you with a male body, you would have become a sensuous woman instead of the dried-up, uptight prude you are!"

Marnie stared at her face in the mirror over her dressing table. It had recently marked its thirtieth year but was still as smooth and wrinkle-free as a teenager's. The only feature that lent it maturity were the eyes. From the day she was born they had viewed the world solemnly.

Or so it seemed.

That's why Law thought she was a prude. She'd always had that effect on people. Through childhood and young adulthood she'd been ridiculed for being so straight, so dull, so *serious*.

Did anyone actually think she liked having an overactive conscience? She didn't. It was boring. She hadn't enjoyed being the party pooper all her life. But someone had

had to be. And since Sharon was the hell-raiser in the family, it had fallen to Marnie to be the chaperone.

Sighing, she switched out the lamp, moved toward her solitary bed, and shrugged off her robe. Lightly her hands skimmed over her nightgown. Her body was narrow and lean. *Voluptuous* would never apply. Sharon, who had matured early, had started turning men's heads by the time she was twelve, much to their parents' consternation.

In her kinder moments, which had been few and far between, Sharon had promised her despairing younger sister that if she were only patient, she would eventually have cleavage and rounded, womanly hips.

With a rueful smile Marnie slid between the sheets. Those long-anticipated curves had never developed. She'd stopped expecting them years before.

She knew she had a certain allure. Even if her eyes didn't dance and twinkle flirtatiously, they were large and ringed with thick, dark lashes. The shape of her mouth seemed to be particularly attractive to some men.

The sculptor she had posed for—wouldn't Colonel Kincaid be shocked to know that while an art student at the university she had posed nude for a sculptor—had found her mouth intriguing and sexy.

That's what had first aroused him that afternoon when he had left his work, crossed the studio, and, with damp clay still clinging to his fingers, brushed them across her mouth. To her dismay and mortification, her nipples had tightened.

Encouraged, the artist had taken the caress further. He kissed her lips and fondled her small, pointed breasts. She responded. The sculptor had a rather elevated ego and would have been crushed to know that his touch in itself hadn't elicited that sensual response from her body.

It was the memory of Law, laughing at her on the beach as his straight white teeth demolished the peak of a Sno-Kone before it dissolved in the sun. They'd bought the Sno-Kones to toast their sand castle, which had taken a half day to erect.

"Hey, squirt, that Sno-Kone's done a dye job on your lips."

His fingers had been gritty with sand as he dragged them across her syrup-stained lips; and young Marnie Hibbs had experienced sexual desire for the first time in her life.

She hadn't even known how to label that delicious, warm, flowering sensation in her lower body. She hadn't attributed the sudden projection of her nipples against her swimsuit to Law's touch. Only later had she understood what had happened to her that afternoon.

The artist accidentally conjured up that memory. Marnie closed her eyes and pretended that it was Law Kincaid who was kissing her, caressing her, lowering her to a grubby mattress under the eaves of a loft studio and taking her virginity.

Eventually, however, she had opened her eyes. It wasn't Law lying beside her, but a man she barely knew, a man with clay on his fingers and a smug grin on his face. She never went back to his studio, even though every penny she could earn had counted. She had often wondered who the artist had gotten to pose so he could finish the piece.

She didn't have the natural resources to entice a man, especially a sybarite like Law Kincaid. But he would be surprised to know about the yearning turbulence that lay just below her puritanical facade.

His accusation that she was a prude had stung, not because it was true, but because it was so untrue. If David hadn't returned then, if Law hadn't left the pool and hastily stepped into his discarded shorts, she might have proved to him just how sensuous she was.

"No, I wouldn't," she admitted in the dark, not knowing whether to congratulate herself for being strong or reproving herself for being such a coward.

Since she had rebuffed him, she would probably never hear from him again. That would be best for everyone involved. The idea of having a son had probably appealed to him only because he had thought it was a package deal that came complete with an available female.

Let him deal with the problem of the anonymous letters himself. She wanted to have nothing more to do with him.

Before she fell asleep, however, the permissive side of Marnie Hibbs fantasized about the things she would love to do with him.

7

When she heard from him again, it was for a reason she least expected.

"I beg your pardon?" she said into the telephone receiver.

"Can you go or not?"

"Not."

"Why not?"

"For one thing, it's two o'clock in the afternoon. And you said this dinner is at—"

"Eight. It takes six hours to get ready?"

"I don't have anything to wear to an affair like that, Law. Why are you inviting me anyway? Surely you've got a little black book just bulging with names of congenial female companions."

"I'm calling you because it's your fault I don't have a date."

"*My* fault?"

"I've been distracted since I met David. I forgot about the damn dinner until somebody here in the office mentioned it a few minutes ago."

"I'm awfully sorry. You can skip it, you can take someone else, or you can go alone, but it's really not my problem that you're stuck without a date."

"It's practically required that I go, and I'll never hear the end of it from the guys around here if I show up without a date."

"Bad for your image?"

"Yes. So is the sudden appearance of a son I didn't know I had," he added in a quieter voice. He was calling her from his office at the space center. "I had the blood test and it matched David's. We need to talk, Marnie. Come with me tonight, please."

Gnawing on her lip, she glanced at the project she was under a deadline to finish by the end of the week. She caught her reflection in the mirror. Everything would require a major overhaul before she could possibly attend a black-tie dinner.

She cited those excuses to Law, then added bleakly, "And I've got to visit my mother this afternoon."

"You're a capable lady. I'll pick you up at eight-fifteen."

"I thought it started at eight?"

"You don't expect me to arrive on time, do you?"

·　　·　　·

"What do you think?" Marnie asked worriedly.

"You look sensational!" David exclaimed from behind her. Together they analyzed her image in the mirror on her closet door.

She turned to her right, then her left. "Is the dress too much?"

"Too much? It's almost too *little*."

"David," she cried anxiously, "you said before that it wasn't that low cut."

He laughed. "It's not. I was just kidding."

Between the hairdresser, where she got coiffed and manicured, and an uneventful visit to the rest home, she'd gone against her better judgment and stopped at an expensive dress shop. In rapid succession she had dismissed several formal dresses as being inappropriate for one reason or another.

She was beginning to lose heart, when she spotted this one. The bodice was electric-blue satin, strapless, and body-hugging. Beneath it was a short, sassy bubble skirt of black satin.

"Honey, if you don't walk out of here with that, I'm gonna cry," the owner of the shop had told her.

"Do you think it's too . . . too . . . fancy for me?"

"It's perfect! Truly."

When the saleswoman was required to ring up a sale for another customer, Marnie discreetly checked the price tag on the dress and almost exclaimed her distress out loud. Giving herself one last, wistful glance in the three-way mirror, she went back into the dressing room and began unzipping it.

The saleswoman rejoined her. "MasterCard or Visa?"

"Neither, I'm afraid. I can't take it."

"Honey, why not? It looks absolutely stunning on you."

"I can't afford it. I can't afford even to charge it," she replied, passing the dress to the woman and slipping her street clothes back on.

The saleswoman plucked a ballpoint pen from behind her ear and made a slash through the price, scribbling something else. "There, does that make it more affordable?"

Marnie looked at the adjustment. "That's half price!"

"It just went on sale."

"But I can't let—"

"Listen, honey, this merchandise was marked up a hundred percent anyway. Even at this price, I'll still make a profit. Just about everybody's bought their spring formals already. Besides, I don't have many customers who wear a size two. It was dumb of me to buy it in such a small size. I'm glad to sell it at any price."

So Marnie had purchased the dress and was now modeling it for her son before her escort arrived. She was as jittery as a girl on prom night.

"I just wish I had more, you know, up here," she said regretfully as her hand made a sweep across her chest.

"Really, Mom, whether or not a girl has boobs isn't a big deal to guys anymore."

She met David's eyes in the mirror. "Now try repeating that with a straight face."

He was grinning sheepishly when the doorbell pealed. "Truly, Mom, you look great!" he shouted over his shoulder as he bounded out of the room and raced for the stairs.

She had loyal David's admiration, but what would Law, who was accustomed to escorting much younger, much curvier women, think of the uptight prude tonight?

He looked positively scrumptious. Better than Death by Chocolate, her favorite dessert. He was wearing a military tuxedo. The epaulets enhanced his broad shoulders. The short white jacket hugged his narrow waist. And what the dark slacks did for his buns was as sinful as asking for extra almonds on Death by Chocolate.

He whistled as she came down the stairs. "Doesn't she look terrific?" David asked.

"Not bad," Law drawled in a voice that made her exposed knees go weak and her exposed décolletage flutter.

"We'll be back around . . . when, Law?"

"Don't wait up," Law told David with a broad wink.

"I won't leave the porch light on either," he said.

"You will so!" Marnie sternly instructed. "Leave all the outdoor lights on and keep the doors locked. Don't answer the door unless—"

"Mom!" he said, rolling his eyes ceilingward. "I'm not a kid, you know."

"I know." She placed her hand on his arm and gave it an affectionate squeeze. "G'night."

"G'night, David." Law escorted Marnie out the door and down the walkway.

"Say, Law?"

"Yeah?" He stopped, turned. David motioned him back. They had a brief whispered exchange before David stepped back into the house and latched the door as he'd been told.

Law was grinning as he helped Marnie into the low seat of the Porsche. "What was that about?" she asked when he slid behind the wheel.

"Man talk."

"I want to know."

"No, you don't," he said, chuckling.

"Yes, I do."

"You sure?"

"Yes."

He pulled up at the stop sign at the end of their block and looked at her across the console. "He told me that if I wanted to take you to bed I had his permission. He promised not to punch me out."

"Go ahead, try it." Law was urging her to eat a raw oyster.

"They're repulsive. No thanks."

He tipped the shell to his lips and swallowed the slimy thing whole. She shuddered. He laughed. "They're good for you, supposed to increase your virility."

"That would be lost on me, since I'm not virile in the first place."

"I noticed that," he said, his eyes taking in the low-cut top of her dress.

Blushing, she tried to distract his fixed stare. "Better watch it. Suzette will get jealous."

"Who?"

Marnie nodded in the direction of the sultry, voluptuous blonde. She was wearing a red leather mini-dress and decorating the arm of a recently divorced NASA administrator.

"Oh, her," Law remarked indifferently, bringing his head back around to Marnie. "She's just a groupie."

"I was talking with her earlier. She says you stood her up last week."

"That's right."

"Heartless jerk."

"It was your fault."

"Why are all your recent travails with women my fault?" she asked.

"I had a date with her the day I met David. I didn't feel much like going out that night."

"I see."

"You don't have to smile about it," he grumbled, noticing that her lips had curved upward. In fact, since picking her up, he had divided his attention between her mouth and her neckline in such a way as to make her stomach jumpy.

"It gives us peons enormous pleasure to watch the mighty topple," she teased.

"How'd you get to know Suzette anyway?"

"We got acquainted while you and your buddies were talking about the A-3."

"You mean the A-4?"

"I mean the A-4. Suzette said . . . what exactly *is* an A-4?"

"A navy jet trainer. Sometimes I strap one on and take it out for a spin."

"You take a military plane out for a spin?" Having such gall was inconceivable to her.

"I've gotta keep my test-pilot skills well honed," he said defensively.

She studied him, her expression pensive. "Why do you love flying so much?"

They had tacitly selected this private spot on the deck overlooking a man-made canal as the place to nibble from their plates of hors d'oeuvres. The waterway was edged with azaleas in full bloom, making the bank look like a giant fuchsia caterpillar. A wisteria vine trailed along the railing of the deck, its lavender blooms dripping toward the water.

The night was balmy. While most of the guests milled through the rooms of their hosts' spectacular home, laughing and chatting with one another over the music of a five-piece ensemble, Marnie and Law sat together on a bench outside.

"I love the exhilaration I feel up there. The higher I can go, and the faster, the more I love it."

"Is your mother still afraid for you?"

He cocked his head to one side. "How did you know that?"

"You referred to it in Galveston. I remember the day. It

rained one afternoon, so we got up a game of Monopoly. Sharon lost interest and went to take a nap."

"Your mom and dad were napping too," he said. "We were by ourselves on that screened porch that overlooked the beach."

Marnie was pleased that he remembered. "You told me all about your plans to apply for the astronaut program after you'd served your stint in the regular navy. That's when you told me your mother was afraid for you to fly those fighter jets and test planes."

"Well, she still is. While I was on the space shuttle mission, Dad said he wanted to keep her sedated, but she stayed glued to the TV and radio."

"I can relate to that," Marnie said softly.

She had done virtually the same thing. During that week she had gotten very little work done and even less sleep. Sick with worry, she had prowled the rooms of her house, her mind cruelly replaying the *Challenger* explosion. She remembered weeping with relief when Law landed the shuttle at Edwards Air Force Base, bringing the successful mission to an end.

"Mother is almost as afraid of space as she is that I'll never get married and have—" He broke off and glanced out over the water.

"Have children?"

His eyes swung back to Marnie. "The blood tests didn't prove that I'm David's father. But they proved that I *could* be." In an even softer voice he added, "I believe I am."

"You are. Sharon was a virgin."

"Are you sure?" His brow was beetled with intensity and the need to be positive.

"Oh, yes," Marnie answered, giving a sad little laugh. "She confided everything to me. If she'd had a lover before you, I would have known about it. She thought it was neat that her first lover was an older man with so much prior experience."

"I don't remember her very well," he confessed. "She's just this vague blur in my memory. Good body. Long blond hair. An easy lay." He studied Marnie's face in the flickering light reflecting off the water. "I remember more about you than about Sharon."

"I find that very hard to believe, Law."

"It's the truth. We talked quite a lot, didn't we?"

"You talked. I listened."

He shook his head and laughed with chagrin. "I guess I was pretty full of myself."

"And I was in awe. I was nothing but a scrawny kid who tagged along and was sent away whenever you and Sharon wanted to make out. Miss Goody-Two-Shoes, remember?"

His grin was slow in coming and lazy when it got there. His eyes lowered to the tops of her breasts, which made small half-moons above her neckline. "This is Miss Goody-Two-Shoes' coming-out party. Literally."

Flustered, she nodded toward the lighted rooms. "They're calling everyone inside for dinner." Raising his left arm, she consulted his wristwatch. "And it's about time too. Ten-thirty! That's not dinnertime. That's bedtime."

He rotated his hand so that his palm slid against hers and he clasped her fingers warmly. His other arm slipped around her waist. "That can be arranged."

She took a breath that caused the half-moons to quaver. "Be serious, Law."

"I'm dead serious. Men always remember the ones that got away, you know. I'm just dying to find out what makes Miss Goody-Two-Shoes so damned good."

Marnie didn't want to be thinking about anything except Law when he was holding her this close. But her conscientious mind wouldn't let her enjoy his embrace. It was dwelling on the results of the blood tests and Law's softly spoken confirmation that David was his.

"Will you tell your parents that they have a grandchild?" She felt the sudden tensing in his muscles. And though his smile was still in place, it no longer looked natural.

"I don't know."

"Knowing that David is yours, what are you going to do, Law?"

He withdrew his arms and stood, offering her a hand up. "You're right, they're calling everybody in for dinner. We'd better not keep them waiting."

As he ushered her through the terrace doors, he leaned over and whispered, "I'll say this for you, Marnie, you know how to deflate what had promised to be good, hard arousal."

8

He rang her doorbell at eleven o'clock the following day. She was surprised to see him. The night before, his attitude toward her had been tense and guarded from the moment they rejoined the party after their conversation outside on the deck.

When he walked her to her front door, he had told her a terse good-night and given her a perfunctory kiss that indicated he was glad to see a conclusion to the evening. That's why this visit was so unexpected.

"Are you busy?" he asked through the screen door.

"I'm working."

She smelled like acrylic paint and looked like the dickens. Her salon hairdo hadn't survived the night. Her hair was back to the loose, short curls that carelessly surrounded her small head. The formal dress had been zipped into a garment bag and hung in the cedar closet. This morning she had dressed in a pair of shorts and a shirt that were far from glamorous. Both had been relegated to her work-clothes drawer last summer. They were smeared with paint. She was barefoot.

"May I come in?"

She hesitated for only a second, then unlatched the screen door and pushed it open. "Why aren't you at work?" she asked as they moved down the hallway toward the back of the house.

He dropped into one of the wicker chairs and peeled off his sunglasses. "I was, but a simulator we were working with developed a glitch. We weren't doing anything except standing around telling dirty jokes and waiting for the technicians to find the bug, which they finally announced would probably take until sometime tomorrow. So I took the rest of the day off. What's that?" He pointed his sunglasses at the painting she was working on.

"The cover for a jewelry store catalog. Like it?" She held it up for his inspection. It was a painting of a giant lotus blossom set against a black background. In the center of the milky petals was a cache of glittering gems.

"Different."

"How diplomatic," she said dryly. "I'm glad the ad agency has already approved my sketch or I'd be worried." He smiled wanly, as though he weren't really listening. "Is something on your mind, Law?"

"Lunch."

"Lunch?"

"Let me take you to lunch," he said abruptly.

"No! I'm a mess."

"You look fine."

"Forget it. I'm not going out looking like this."

"Okay, then we'll lunch in. What have you got?"

Before she could say another word, he was disappearing through the doorway into the kitchen. By the time she reached it, he was bent at the waist, taking inventory of the refrigerator.

She crossed the room and rudely pushed the refrigerator door shut. "You didn't come here to eat."

He leaned back against the refrigerator and gazed up at the ceiling. "You're right. I didn't."

"So why are you here?"

"I keep thinking about what you asked me last night. What am I going to do about David?"

Marnie felt that squeezing little pressure around her heart that she experienced each time she thought about what action Law might take regarding David.

Softly, almost fearfully, she asked, "Have you decided?"

"No," he answered, bringing his eyes down to her level. "Not yet. Before I do anything about the future, I've got to catch up on the past."

She shook her head, puzzled. "I don't understand."

"I like what I see now. By all appearances, he's a super kid, all a father could hope for in a son. I'd like to know how he got that way. God, I've missed so much. There are sixteen years of life that I know absolutely nothing about except that he couldn't have a dog because pets made his grandmother nervous and that he took swimming lessons at the Y."

His expression was bleak and full of appeal. "Tell me how it was, Marnie. Stuff me with information."

She glanced toward her work area, which beckoned, but reasoned that she could burn the midnight oil if necessary to get the piece finished under her deadline.

"Come with me." She led him from the kitchen into the living room, where she kept photo albums chock-full of snapshots of David.

Her emotions were mixed. Difficult as it was to admit, she admired Law for taking an interest in David. He could have gotten furious when he learned of David's existence. Even after acknowledging that it was possible he had fathered him, he could have shrugged him off as a biological fluke as most men who dated girls named Suzette would have.

But then, Law Kincaid was a higher caliber man than most. He had earned a congressional appointment to the Naval Academy. His life had been studded with achievements and honors. He had the integrity to support his record of successes.

His strong character made her love him that much more, but it also made him her enemy. Anonymous threatening letters notwithstanding, he wasn't a man who would blithely turn his back on a teenage son. It had been Marnie's selfish wish that that's what he would do.

Until he revealed what, if any, his plans for the future were, she was blindly feeling her way through the situation. For the time being, cooperating with him was the best strategy.

She sat down cross-legged on the floor and pulled a large picture album onto her lap. Law dropped down beside her. She opened the cover of the album and smoothed her hand over the certificate pasted to the first page.

"His official footprints, done soon after he was born."

Law's eyes lit up. "So tiny!"

"Not the size elevens they are now," she said, laughing. "They look so sweet here, but whenever I clear out his dirty clothes hamper, his gym socks don't smell so sweet. It amazes me now to think that I once nibbled on his toes."

On the next page were pictures of the day the Hibbs family had brought David home from the hospital. Law studied a photograph of Sharon holding her new son. "She doesn't look overjoyed with him."

"She'd just given birth," Marnie remarked charitably. "She wasn't feeling too well."

He stripped away her sugar coating. "She didn't really want him, did she?"

"Well, she—"

"Marnie."

"No, she didn't," she confessed around a deep breath.

"Since you thwarted her abortion plans, why didn't she give him up for adoption?"

"That was her second suggestion, but my parents opposed the idea."

"Why?"

"I think Dad wanted to make a point, teach the moral lesson that one must be held accountable for his or her mistakes."

"One reaps what he sows. I didn't know anybody still adhered to that belief."

"Dad did. He wanted Sharon to learn it the hard way."

"I believe you and they suffered as much if not more than she."

"Dad's ministry was over as soon as word got around that his unmarried daughter was pregnant. Whatever influence he had over the souls of his congregation had been nullified."

"Did that make him resent David?"

"Of course not. David wasn't the transgression, only the product of it. Mom and Dad loved David and were very affectionate toward him. He wouldn't be as well adjusted as he is if they hadn't been."

"How did your dad earn a living after that?" he asked as he turned the pages of the album, studying each picture of David at some length.

"He went to work for a publisher of religious books."

"And died of a heart attack."

"Hmm. Mother took it hard. Especially since his death came so close on the heels of Sharon's accident."

"What happened, Marnie?"

"I told you. An accident. A car wreck, to be specific."

He placed his finger beneath her chin and turned her face toward his. They were sitting very close, their shoulders touching. Her knee was resting on his thigh. She suddenly became aware of that, though she didn't remember how it had gotten there.

"Be *more* specific."

"It doesn't matter now. David doesn't remember," she said evasively.

"I'm waiting."

She closed her eyes and whispered, "She was drunk. Her car crossed the center stripe and hit another car head-on. There were two people in it. All three of them were killed on impact."

He swore liberally, out of anger and regret. Intuitively Marnie realized what he was thinking, and consolingly laid her hand on his thigh.

"It wasn't your fault, Law. You never even knew that she got pregnant. Don't start blaming yourself for deserting a girl you got in trouble. Sharon got herself in trouble, and if it hadn't been with you, it would have been with someone else.

"She was a rebel from the day she realized that Dad was a minister and therefore exemplary behavior was expected of her. She resented that and in retaliation flaunted her misdeeds. She was the source of constant disharmony within our family. Her conduct made our parents very unhappy.

And though it broke their hearts, I doubt they were even surprised when she got pregnant."

"Why didn't they contact me or my parents?"

"Sharon told them she didn't know who the father was. She boasted that she'd been sleeping with lots of men. I saw no point in naming you. There were already too many lives affected; why should yours have been ruined too?

"After David was born," she continued, "Sharon refused to go back to high school, saying it was dopey and she was done with all that. Dad insisted that if she didn't return to school, she had to get a job, but she was unskilled and uninterested and kept getting fired."

"What about men?"

"She attracted them, naturally. Motherhood had only ripened her figure." Marnie studied her hands, clenching and unclenching her fingers. "Unfortunately they were the wrong kind of men. My parents grieved to see her squandering her life, but their efforts to control her were ineffectual. Sometimes she'd go out and not come back for days."

"She didn't give a damn about David, did she?"

"No," Marnie said with a sad shake of her head. "She didn't give a damn about anything except creating chaos."

"What does he know about me?"

"Nothing!" she answered in alarm.

"I mean about his father in general. He's a bright boy. Surely he asked."

"Almost as early as he could talk. Just as he told you the

other night, we explained that his father couldn't marry his mother. That it was impossible."

"Didn't he pester you for at least a name?"

"We told him that giving him that was impossible too."

"He didn't demand to know why?"

"We kept the reasons vague and emphasized that he'd be smothered in so much love he wouldn't miss having a father."

"Did he buy that?"

"Probably not. But eventually he accepted it."

"He didn't have much choice, did he?" Law's lips formed a thin, bitter line. "He didn't have a father. And not much of a mother. Who took care of him while Sharon was out carousing?"

"We, my folks and I, shared that privilege."

He gave her a long, steady stare before continuing to turn the pages of the album. "Uh-huh," he said after several minutes. "*You* took care of him, didn't you?"

"I told you, we—"

"Don't make excuses for them," he said harshly. "Look at these pictures. You and David in the park on a picnic. You and David on a merry-go-round, flying a kite, playing with a Frisbee, at Astroworld. Is this his first bicycle?"

"Christmas morning, when he was five," she said, smiling down at the group of photographs. They featured a younger version of David wearing Smurf pajamas and pushing a shiny bicycle through a sea of wrapping paper.

"I wanted to leave the training wheels on, but he insisted

that I take them off. He wanted to learn to ride it without them."

Law did some swift calculations. "That was the Christmas I spent in the Philippines. Some buddies and I were feeling blue about not being home for Christmas. We went into the nearest town and got plastered.

"And while I was stumbling around under banyan trees looking for a place to puke up cheap vodka, my five-year-old son was half a world away, learning how to ride a bike without the training wheels." He rubbed his fingertips over one of the photographs. "Tough little cuss."

"And stubborn. And impatient with himself," Marnie said. "He always wants to do things right the first time and gets extremely upset if he doesn't. But he sticks with it. He had mastered the bike by the middle of that afternoon."

"Yeah? Really?" Law asked, smiling proudly.

There was a close-up picture of David snarling at the camera, showing where two front teeth were missing, and a somber David all dressed up, with his hair evenly parted, a Bible under his arm. "The day he was baptized," Marnie told his father.

"He went to Sunday school?"

"He still does. He's president of the youth group at our church." She turned another page. "That was his first Little League team. The Pirates."

"What position does he play?"

"Anything in the infield, but baseball's his least favorite sport. Not physical enough, he says."

"It's my least favorite too."

"And these are all his class pictures in chronological order. I didn't know it was picture day until after the fact," she said with asperity as she pointed at one of the photos. "He'd forgotten to bring home the note. I could have killed him for wearing that tacky T-shirt to have his picture taken."

"Oops, one slid out." Law leaned over and picked up the loose photograph. "Must belong on the baptism page. David's all dressed up. But that looks like a judge, not a minister."

"It is a judge. That's the day—"

Law looked at her curiously when she suddenly broke off. "The day what?"

"Nothing."

"What?" He clasped her hands together on the open album so she couldn't busy them to deliberately distract him. "The day what?"

It was impossible for her to look him straight in the eye. "The day the court granted me legal custody of him."

The resulting stillness was broken only by the sound of their breathing. Finally Law said, "You make it sound like that was quite a feat."

"It took several years. I had applied right after Sharon died."

"But you were only eighteen then, weren't you?" She nodded. He blew out a gust of air and muttered a series of blue words. "You reared my son, didn't you? Almost single-handedly. You did what your slut of a sister—"

"Law, don't!"

"I'm not as nice as you, Marnie. She was a slut, and I knew it the minute I laid eyes on her. I did what any young man would have done with a ripe, good-looking girl who was giving it away. She asked for it and she got it. But you're the one who paid for what we did."

"I didn't *pay*," she cried in protest. "I loved David from the day I knew Sharon had conceived him."

"Your folks were too caught up in their own misery or too busy blaming themselves for Sharon's behavior, so they abdicated the responsibility of taking care of David to you."

"It wasn't something they did consciously. It just evolved that way. And I didn't look upon David as a responsibility. I wanted to mother him."

"And you did from the very beginning, didn't you?"

"The house was in constant turmoil. There were so many hard feelings between Sharon and my parents, so much—"

"Who got up with him in the middle of the night?"

"I did," she said quietly.

"You changed him, gave him his bottle?"

"Yes."

"God, you were only a kid yourself."

"He didn't know that." She was smiling radiantly, but her eyes were glistening with tears. "He didn't know any more about being a baby than I did about being a mother. We tolerated each other and learned together."

"You poked that gunk that babies have to eat into his mouth."

"And what he didn't like, he spat out."

"You bandaged his skinned knees."

"The knees weren't so bad, but he was hell on elbows."

"What about your schooling?"

"I went. I even graduated from college. It took me a little longer, that's all."

"Because you could handle only a light class load because you didn't want to leave David for long with your mother during the day," he said, guessing correctly.

"Yes, but—"

"And when you had your degree, you didn't even try for a well-paying position with an advertising firm as you could have. You opted to work at home so you would be here for David, right?"

"There were other considerations."

"I doubt it." Law closed his eyes and leaned forward until his forehead was resting against hers. "You made all the parental sacrifices. *You* are his mother, Marnie. You."

"The only way David could be more mine is if I'd been on that beach blanket with you instead of Sharon."

He pulled back quickly. Marnie was equally stunned by her own words, but she didn't move. She didn't even blink, only returned his stare with serious gray eyes. As he watched, a tear trickled down her cheek.

He whisked it away, then rubbed his wet thumb across

her lips. "If I had it to do over again, you would be. You're twice the woman she was."

His fingers closed around her head and drew her face up to his. He kissed the dewy spot the tear had left on her cheekbone, then the corner of her lips.

"I wanted to do that last night so badly my gut ached," he whispered roughly. He kissed the other corner of her mouth. "You want to know why I'm here today? This is why. Every time you smiled at somebody I introduced you to last night, every time you took a sip of wine, every time you took a bite of food, I wanted to be tasting your beautiful, sexy mouth. And that chaste, obligatory good-night kiss at your front door only whetted my appetite."

His lips had been resting against hers during the arousing speech. Now he flicked his tongue against the seam of her lips. Marnie made an involuntary yearning sound. Law applied more pressure and nudged her lips apart. His tongue, sleek and agile and swift, mated with hers. She allowed it, and even participated eagerly.

"Damn," he groaned when he finally pulled back. "I should have kissed you right a long time ago."

Marnie welcomed his lips again and the sweet, warm dampness of his kiss. Responding to the hungry, rapid tempo he set and her own sensuous impulses, she slipped her arms around his waist and hugged him close. He went up on his knees and pulled her to him, so that they were kneeling and facing each other.

His lips left a trail of quick hot kisses down her throat,

then, brushing aside the collar of her shirt, he planted a solid one at its base.

She threw her head back and gasped his name.

"Touch me, Marnie." Taking her hand, he thrust it beneath his shirt and flattened it against the fuzzy warmth of his chest.

He frantically began undoing the buttons of her shirt but, when they were undone, sat back on his heels, surprised to find that she wasn't wearing a bra. Modestly she tried to pull her shirt together, but he pushed aside her anxious hands and gazed at her lustfully.

Misgivings assailed her. All were dispelled the instant he lowered his blond head and kissed the slope of one breast, hoarsely whispering her name as she had often heard it in her dreams.

She mindlessly caressed him, her hand lightly riding his ribs. Her thumb made accidental but electrifying contact with his distended nipple. He hissed a curse and gently nipped her breast.

"I can't believe this is happening." She wasn't aware she'd spoken her thoughts aloud until Law responded by drawing her closer and mumbling against her flesh. "It is. I can feel you, taste you."

His body was the finest work of art Marnie had ever experienced. She wanted to savor it, to indulge her appreciation of it, but his lips were sweeping kisses across her breasts and setting an erotic pace that wasn't conducive to dalliance.

His tongue stroked her nipple again and again. Her free

hand cupped the back of his head as his mouth closed around the raised center and tugged on it with a demanding appetite.

"Law." His name escaped her lips on a long, low moan.

"I know. I know. I'm hurting too."

He pushed her hand down to his trousers. He was firm and full. Marnie froze. Law didn't notice. He reached for the button on her shorts, and when it was undone, he pulled down the zipper.

Feeling the cool metal rasp against her skin abruptly snapped Marnie out of her trance and woke her up to exactly what this was leading to.

"No, Law," she said suddenly, pushing him away. She struggled to stand up, tripped over a photo album, and broke her fall against the arm of an upholstered chair.

Law, at a complete loss, didn't quite make it to his feet, but flopped back into the seat of the chair she'd stumbled into. He stared up at her with incomprehension as she grappled with the uncooperative buttons of her blouse.

"This is crazy," she said in a shaky voice. "Groping on the living room floor like—"

She had given up on the buttons. Her fingers wouldn't work properly while he was sitting there staring at her exposed torso. Her only alternative was to leave the room with as much dignity as possible.

She almost made it past the chair. But his arm shot out and his fingers shackled her wrist and drew her back between his widely spread knees.

"Law, we can't."

"The hell we can't," he growled, and he flipped open her shirt and pressed his open mouth against her bare stomach.

Marnie nearly fainted from the sheer eroticism of the embrace. She clasped his head in an attempt to regain her balance, but when her fingers knotted in his hair, it ended up being a caress.

His mouth was warm and wet and wonderful. And active. He loosely clasped her waist and nibbled at the fragile, sensitive skin of her belly, working his way down. His tongue flirted with her navel as his hands moved behind her to palm her derriere.

His beard stubble abraded her. His breath felt damp. His teeth were sharp, his tongue soft. The delicious sensations came in rapid succession. They were new, thrilling in contrast, and each more exquisite than the one before it.

His chin inched down the elastic waistband of her underpants. He kissed the paler skin beneath her bikini tan line. But when she felt his lips make contact with the cloud of dark hair, she caught her breath sharply.

"Law, what are you doing?"

"What does it feel like?"

What it felt like was too marvelous to describe and too scandalous to permit. Weak with desire, miserable with love, Marnie forced herself to push him away again. This time she stepped well out of his reach.

9

She was waiting by the front door when he came out of the living room. Her clothing, if not her composure, had been restored. "I think you'd better go," she said coldly.

"I think you'd better grow up."

She curbed her fury. Confrontations had never been enjoyable or easy for her. "Simply because I don't want to be manhandled on the living room floor is no reason for you to be insulting."

"What bothers you the most? The handling?" He hooked his thumbs through his belt loops and assumed an arrogant stance. "Or the man?"

Her mouth dropped open. "Just what are you implying, Law?"

"Nothing," he said with a nonchalant shrug. "I'll be in touch."

He started to go past her, but she grabbed his arm. "I

think you are implying something. And it's totally un-founded."

"Unfounded?" His eyes, so fluid and feverish with passion only minutes before, were now brittle and disparaging. "Why do you freeze up every time a man touches you?"

"I don't!"

"You sure as hell can't prove it by me!" he shouted. "Why haven't you ever been married?"

"That's none of your business."

"It damn sure is. You've got custody of my son, so I have every right to know everything there is to know about you, even your most personal secrets." He stepped closer, deliberately putting her on the defensive. "Why aren't you married?"

"No one has ever asked me."

"I don't doubt that. You freeze a guy in his boots if he so much as thinks the word *sex*. If you loved David as much as you claim—"

"I do."

"Then why didn't you marry for his sake, just so there would be a man around? Unless, of course, the thought of sleeping with a man is so repugnant to you that not even David's welfare could overcome it." His blue eyes narrowed. "I'm not sure you've created a very healthy climate for my son, Miss Hibbs."

"Oh, and I suppose that pleasure palace you call a house would be a much healthier environment, where babes like Suzette come and go at will. How healthy would it be for a teenage boy to know that his father has a swimsuit on hand to fit every size and shape female?"

"At least my lifestyle is *normal*."

"Sickeningly normal, Colonel Kincaid. Just like it was normal for you to imply there is something wrong with *me* because I said no to having a nooner on the living room floor, which was only something exciting to occupy you on an afternoon when you've got idle time on your hands."

She paused and drew a deep breath. "Well, for your information, I'm busy. So take your boredom, which I'm certain is what prompted you to come here in the first place, and your lewd insinuations about my sexuality, and leave my house."

He did, but not before tossing a subtle threat over his retreating shoulder. "This isn't the end of this thing. Not by a long shot."

"That's really neat, Grandma. Thanks."

David graciously accepted the key chain Mrs. Hibbs had made for him over a period of weeks in the morning crafts class. The nursing home had daily scheduled activities. Marnie was glad to know that her mother had been feeling well enough to participate in some of them, even if the aides had done most of the handiwork on the key chain.

"I know your birthday is coming up." Her speech was slow but understandable. "Maybe you can use it."

"I can. It's great," David claimed. The plastic disk had

his name painstakingly painted on it. He bounced it in his palm. "Thanks again."

"You'll be careful when you start to drive, won't you?" Mrs. Hibbs asked anxiously. "I think about Sharon."

Marnie laid a comforting hand on her mother's shoulder. "David's very conscientious, Mother."

"I'll be careful, Grandma. Mom would have a cow if I wasn't. And I know the consequences of drinking and driving."

Mrs. Hibbs seemed reassured. She relaxed in the chair beside her bed, the one that had been moved from the house. It personalized and gave a touch of homeyness to the otherwise clinical room.

"Are you tired, Mother?" Marnie asked. Mrs. Hibbs was always glad to see David, but even his presence in the small room exhausted her. His youthful energy seemed to vacuum up the oxygen.

"A little. But don't go yet."

"Why don't you wait outside, David, while I help Grandma get settled for the night? Then you can come back in to say good-bye."

"Okay. That's fine," David said quickly. He never quarreled about paying his grandmother visits, but Marnie knew that he didn't enjoy coming to the rest home. He couldn't relate to infirmity and old age and found the grim reality of them distressing.

Marnie spent the next fifteen minutes preparing her mother for the night. A nurse came in with her evening medication. In only minutes the sleeping pill took effect and Mrs. Hibbs dozed off.

Marnie opened her mother's nightstand drawer to replace some grooming articles. That's when she saw the box of stationery, the ballpoint pen, and the book of postage stamps. For a moment she stared at them, curious to know who her mother could be corresponding with. She hadn't asked Marnie to bring her the stationery. Nor had she asked for any assistance in writing letters.

Then the horrifying realization struck her.

Mrs. Hibbs was softly snoring, her chest rising and falling evenly. But even in repose her face didn't look peaceful. There was a groove of discontent between her eyebrows, and her lips were pulled down at the corners. She was dying a very unhappy woman.

Marnie left the room and went directly to the nurses' station. "Excuse me," she said, addressing the woman on duty, "has my mother been sending out letters lately?"

The nurse smiled. "We're so proud of her. It's very difficult for her to write, you know. Sometimes it takes her days to compose one, but she's been sending out about one letter a week for several weeks now." Then, noticing the anxiety on Marnie's face, she asked, "Is something wrong?"

"I don't suppose you noticed whom the letters were addressed to?"

"No, I'm sorry. But then, it really wasn't my business."

"Of course not. No. Thank you."

She turned and thoughtfully made her way back down the

corridor. "Hey, Mom, where've you been?" David asked as he rounded a corner and almost ran into her. "I went in to say good night, but Grandma—what's the matter?"

Marnie shook her head vaguely. "Nothing. I . . . uh, nothing. Let's go."

Once at home, she tried to work on the jewelry catalog cover, but couldn't concentrate. Her conscience was too busy. She couldn't be positive, but it seemed very likely that her mother had sent the letters to Law. Much as she dreaded the thought of facing him, she knew he should be apprised immediately. And he should be told in person.

Tossing down her brush and recapping her paints, she went upstairs, freshened up, and then went into David's bedroom. He was propped against the headboard of his bed, a history book lying open in his lap and a Walkman bridging his head. He removed the headpiece when he saw Marnie standing in the doorway.

"Huh?"

"Ma'am," she gently corrected.

"Ma'am?"

"I've got to run an errand."

He glanced at his bedside clock. "It's almost ten o'clock."

"I know. I won't be long."

"Where're you going? To the store? Can I go? I'll drive."

"No, I'm not going to the store."

"Then where? What's up, Mom? Did something happen with Grandma?"

"No, it's nothing like that. Studying for an exam?"

"Yeah, but—"

"If I'm not back before you're ready to go to bed, make sure the doors are locked."

"Okay." He was frowning. "I wish you'd tell me what's going on."

"Nothing for you to worry about." She blew him a kiss and left before he could pose any more questions that she'd have to answer with lies.

On the drive to Law's house, she rehearsed what she was going to say. She wanted to keep it simple and to the point. After what had happened earlier that day, it was going to be uncomfortable to be alone with him.

But being alone with him looked doubtful. The minute she turned onto his street she noticed the line of cars parked along both curbs. Loud music was pouring from his house. He was obviously hosting a party.

Her first impulse was to go home. The news could wait. But before she could back into a driveway to turn her car around, she changed her mind.

She had spent a miserable afternoon trying to decide whether she was glad she'd called a halt to their lovemaking or whether she regretted it. She hadn't been able to work. She'd been restless and irritable. The day had been far from pleasant. It was irksome to her that Law could have survived their angry scene unscathed and in a party mood.

So, parking her car, she walked up the petunia-bordered path to the privacy fence gate that she knew led to the backyard. There were several guests frolicking in the pool and stewing in the hot tub. The deck was thronged with people. It was an eclectic crowd.

As she moved through it, she was ogled by two cowboys, each of whom was caressing a Suzette clone with one hand while lifting a can of beer to his lips with the other.

She was ignored by a group of executive types who were drinking whiskey and lamenting the dropping price of Texas crude. She caught the tail end of a rank story about a traveling salesman and a lady mud wrestler.

When she stepped on something squishy, she looked down to find that it was a sodden bikini bra. She didn't want to know where it had come from or where the bottom was.

"Ma'am?"

She turned to find a man sitting yoga fashion in a flower bed of periwinkles. His long straight white hair was held back with a sequined headband, and his eyes were glazed. He was obviously high on the joint he was smoking. "You're blocking my view," he told her solemnly.

"Oh, sorry." She moved on, doggedly wending her way toward the house because she didn't see Law anywhere outside.

It was standing room only in the kitchen. A group of respectable-looking women were analyzing the ingredients of a creamy pink dip and bemoaning the long hours they spent chauffeuring their children around to all their activities. She recognized them as wives of astronauts. She'd met most of them the night of the dinner she'd attended with Law.

A beefy bully with a Mohawk haircut and swastika earring was terrorizing the fish in the aquarium with an empty beer can while humming the ominous tune from *Jaws*.

Around the table, a boisterous group of men were talking flying. Marnie recognized the husbands of the women who had transferred their attention from the creamy pink dip to one's new French-manicured fingernails. Tonight the NASA men had been joined by a few younger military types. All were listening attentively to one of the astronauts.

". . . coming in low like this," he was saying, making a swooping gesture with his hands. "He made a pass to land, but the tower waved him off."

"It did more than wave me off."

The voice belonged to Law, who was straddling a chair backward, his hands folded over its back. There was a woman straddling the seat, too, behind Law, giving his shoulders a massage and his ear a bath with her tongue.

Marnie wanted to cross the room and slap both of them very hard, an urge that stunned her, since previously she hadn't believed she had a violent bone in her entire body. The one and only time she'd ever spanked David, she had cried harder than he.

"The damn cowards were afraid of a little smoke," Law was saying drolly.

"A little smoke? Clouds of black smoke," the first

speaker added. Law shrugged and took a swig of beer from the can sitting on the table in front of him. "Anyhow, this crazy sum'bitch comes around again, ignores the orders to eject and ditch the plane—said later his headset must've gone on the blink—and landed the thing on a dime. A *dime*."

He shook his head in admiration. "Never saw anything like it in all my days of flying. And what'd the brass do to him? Read him the riot act for disobeying orders? Hell no! Not Apollo here. They gave him a damn medal!"

"You've done crazier stunts yourself," Law said over the laughter.

"He certainly has." The astronaut's wife moved up behind him and tipped the bill of his NASA cap over his eyes. "That was before I told him if he didn't stop hotdogging in those T-38s, I was gonna stop hotdogging with him in bed."

That elicited laughter, catcalling, wolf whistles, and assorted prurient comments from everyone within listening distance.

"Speaking of which, honey," she said, leaning down and kissing his cheek, "let's go home and leave the real partying to the young single folks. Two parties in a row is too much for an old broad like me to take."

There was a general rearranging of bodies around the table as several of the couples agreed with her and began drifting toward the door.

One of the wives spotted Marnie and smiled. "Hi." Her

smile was open and friendly. "I didn't get a chance to meet you last night. I'm Kris Campbell. This is my husband, Bob."

"Marnie Hibbs." Between the shoulders of the couple she witnessed Law's sudden reaction to her name. He whipped his head toward them. "Pleased to meet you."

"Did I overhear you tell someone that you're an artist?"

"That's right."

"I'd love to visit with you, but we were on our way out. Maybe some other time."

"I'd like that," Marnie said, responding to the woman's friendliness.

"I was so glad to see Law with someone like you last night. For once he had a date with a woman whose IQ is higher than her bust size. That leads me to believe that he's got a brain after all and not just a—"

"Come on, honey," the astronaut interrupted good-naturedly, nudging his wife through the patio door. "We'll catch you later, Marnie."

After they'd gone, Law called out to her, "Marnie, come on in. What are you drinking? Will one of you gentlemen kindly let the lady have your chair?"

"No thank you to both." Her cheeks were burning with indignation, but she was determined to stand her ground. He was being deliberately obnoxious, trying to see what kind of rise he could get out of her. She wouldn't give him the satisfaction of seeing her either cowed or angry. "I need to talk to you, Law."

The girl sitting behind him squirmed closer and possessively locked her arms around his torso. He gave Marnie a phony, helpless shrug. "As you can see, I'm kinda tied up right now. Why don't you relax and have a good time? Join the party. You're among friends. Everybody," he said loudly, "this is Marnie. Marnie, this is—" He groped his memory for names. "These are some pilots I flew with today."

"Kincaid here said he had to blow off some steam or die," one of them informed Marnie. He was sitting at the table, leering up at her drunkenly. "He said getting off on flying a jet is almost as good as getting off with a woman."

"You Air Force fly-boys don't know when to keep your mouths shut, do you?" Law asked, scowling darkly.

The other pilot wasn't listening. Before she realized what was about to happen, he encircled her waist with his strong arm and pulled her onto his lap.

"You promised us lots of women would be here, Kincaid, but failed to say they'd be as classy as this one."

He flattened his hand low on Marnie's stomach and pulled her back against him while he nuzzled her neck. "I like 'em small like this. The smaller the better. Usually when they're this small on the outside, they're small on the inside."

Law shot out of his chair, dumping the redhead behind him onto the floor. He fixed a murderously icy stare on the pilot and said in a voice just as frosty, "The party's over."

10

The laughter died. So did the party atmosphere. Even Ray Charles was silenced in mid-chorus, though how someone found the sound system switch that quickly, Marnie never knew.

Law's eyes served as blades that cut through the arms binding her. As soon as the flyer released her, she stood up and moved away.

Gradually the tension in the kitchen spilled onto the deck beyond and spread like a gloomy tide. All merriment ceased. The party-makers began to funnel through the gate toward their cars.

"Law?" The redhead had picked herself up from the floor and redraped herself over his right side.

Impatiently he shook her off. "The party's over for you too, sweetheart."

Huffily she flounced away. Before she was even through

the door, however, she had latched onto the inebriated pilot who had unwittingly insulted his host.

"How the hell was I s'pposed to know she was somebody special to 'im, huh?" he muttered as his more sober friends hastily ushered him out. None seemed inclined to wave a red flag at Law's temper.

He shot Marnie a hard glance, then went out onto the deck himself. She gazed around the kitchen. It didn't resemble the spotless room she had seen the last time she'd been there. There wasn't a clear surface in it now. It was littered with used paper plates and napkins, empty bottles and cans. An empty beer can had sunk to the gravel bottom of the fish tank.

Hearing a scratching sound, Marnie moved to a door and opened it. Venus leapt out of a utility room. She crouched and eyed Marnie suspiciously, then, realizing that Marnie was her liberator, she crept forward and sniffed her hand.

"Hey, girl." Marnie patted the dog's head. Within seconds they were friends. Why shouldn't they be comrades? Marnie asked herself wryly. They had their jealousy of Law in common. Every time Marnie thought about the luscious redhead and the smug way Law had smiled whenever she wiggled against him, Marnie wanted to scream.

He reentered the kitchen and slid the glass door closed behind him. "Everybody's out. Happy now?"

"It wasn't my intention to break up your party. If you could have pried yourself away from the redhead long enough for me to say what I have to say, it could have gone on for the rest of the night for all I care."

"Too late now. You snuffed it out and almost caused a brawl."

"That drunken foul-mouth was responsible, not me. You should have ignored him."

He propped his hands on his hips and faced her belligerently. "Excuse me. I thought I was defending your honor. Next time some jerk makes a dirty remark about you, I'll keep my mouth shut and let you enjoy it."

She lowered her forehead into her hand and massaged her temples. Under any circumstances this wouldn't have been an easy meeting. But circumstances couldn't be worse or less conducive to a calm discussion of a volatile subject.

Law placed a bowl of jalapeño dip on the floor for Venus to lap up. She attacked it with gusto. When he straightened up, he fixed Marnie with a hostile glare. "Well, let's have it. What was so all-fired important that you had to see me tonight?"

Nervously she glanced around the kitchen. "Would you like me to help you clean this up?"

"That's what you ruined my party to ask?"

"No," she retorted sharply. "Stop making jokes."

"Then stop stalling. The maid will be well paid to clean up the mess tomorrow. So what's on your mind?"

"The letters."

He gave a quick little motion of his head. "What about them?"

"May I see them?"

"What's the matter? Don't you believe me? Do you think I made them up?"

"May I see them, please?" she asked testily.

"What for?"

"Because I think I know who sent them."

"What the hell's all the hollering about? Where'd everybody go?"

At the sound of the intrusive voice, Marnie spun around. A couple was standing in the connecting doorway, wearing puzzled expressions . . . and very little else.

Suzette had a towel pressed against her chest, under which she had on nothing but a pair of bikini trunks. The mystery of the missing half of the suit had been solved at least. The man had a towel wrapped around his waist.

Marnie turned her back on them and knelt down beside Venus. She took away the bowl of dip and replaced it with a slice of rare roast beef from a deli tray of sandwich meats.

"What's going on, Law?" the man asked. "We just went into one of the bedrooms for a while and—"

"It's okay. The party died a sudden death. Everybody left."

"Where's Mary Jo?"

"She went with one of those F-16 jockeys."

"What? And you let her go?"

"Look, I'm not a marriage counselor, okay?" Law said with diminishing patience. "Since you trucked into the bedroom with Suzy Q, I guess Mary Jo felt free to leave with another man. Now, beat it, will ya? I've got problems of my own."

The couple murmured to each other about how *some* people could be *so* rude as they searched for their clothes out on the deck.

Law, ignoring them, raked a hand through his hair. "I'm hungry. Want some cereal?"

Marnie shook her head. He passed up the leftover party food in favor of a bowl of Cheerios and milk. Since the table was so littered, he stood up to eat, bracing his hips against the countertop.

"Who sent me the letters?" he asked around a huge mouthful.

"I believe it was my mother."

He stopped chewing instantly, swallowed the bite, and gaped at her. "Your mother?"

She explained to him about the stationery she had discovered in the nightstand drawer. "She doesn't have any relatives she would be writing to. Besides, since her stroke, handwriting has been very difficult for her." She paused, then spread her hands. "If I could see the letters, I might be able to determine whether or not she wrote them."

He set down the bowl of cereal and crossed to a built-in desk. The letters were in the lap drawer. There were six in all, bound together by a rubber band. He handed the packet to Marnie. She rolled the rubber band to her wrist and inspected the script on all the envelopes, then scanned the contents of two of them.

"Well?" he asked, having resumed scooping cereal into his mouth.

"It doesn't look like her usual handwriting, but it looks like her handwriting since the stroke. And the stationery is identical to what I found. I'm sure they came from her. The phraseology is hers."

Depleted of energy, Marnie lowered herself into one of the chairs at the table. After reading through all the letters, she looked up at him. He was guzzling orange juice straight from the carafe in the refrigerator.

"I don't know what to say, Law." She had never felt so embarrassed in her life. "I can't believe that my mother would do something this unscrupulous."

He plopped down across the table from her. "I thought you said she didn't know that I was David's father."

"She didn't."

"Obviously she did."

"Obviously," she echoed despondently. "She must have known it for a long time. Maybe she suspected that it was you all along, then when David grew up to look so much like you . . . Your face has been in the news so much since the shuttle flight. . . ."

The situation was so mortifying, she found it near impossible to look him in the face. But she garnered her courage and did. "I'm sorry, Law," she said, her voice husky with emotion.

He leaned back in his chair and massaged Venus behind the ears. Her chin was propped forlornly on his thigh, as though sensing that the topic of conversation was dismal. She gazed at Marnie with sad brown eyes.

"It's not your fault, Marnie," Law told her. "I'm certainly not blaming you."

"I'll confront her about it immediately."

"Don't. She's sick. How can she harm me? She's not a blackmailer by trade. It comes as a relief just to know that I'm not being hounded by a pro."

"I'm relieved that there's no real danger to David."

He thoughtfully continued to play with Venus's ears. "You know, in a bizarre way she probably wanted to be found out. Otherwise she wouldn't have put your address on the envelopes."

"But why would she have done it to begin with?" Marnie asked rhetorically. "She became cynical after Sharon and Dad died. Her disposition isn't what you could describe as rosy. But she's never been spiteful."

"I'm sure she thinks it's time I took my punishment."

"The accountability we were talking about earlier," Marnie mused out loud.

"Right." They were both quiet and reflective for several moments. Finally Law said, "It's the damnedest thing, Marnie, but I'm glad she did it."

"Why?"

"Because of David."

Her mouth went dry. "What about him?"

"I hate to think I could have lived the rest of my life without knowing him."

He studied her gravely and she had a strong premonition that she wasn't going to like what was coming next. She was right.

"I think I owe it to him, and to myself, too, for David and me to spend some time together."

She moistened her lips. "By 'time' you mean——"

"I mean that we should see each other on a regular basis, as frequently as possible. Get to know each other. Spend quality time together. Maybe he could even stay here occasionally."

Her worst nightmare was becoming reality. It was unfolding in this wrecked kitchen, amid the debris and spoiling food. From the instant Law Kincaid had walked back into her life, she had feared that it might eventually come down to this moment.

" 'Quality time'?" she mimicked sweetly. "You must have caught *Oprah* one day and picked up that catchy little phrase, because I'm certain you have no idea what quality time between a parent and child is all about."

"Now, just a——"

"What would be your idea of quality time, Colonel?" she asked, coming out of her chair. "An orgy? Sharing Suzette or one of the other groupies that flock around you? A wild party every night, one where David could invite his friends too?"

"I know that what happened here tonight looks bad, Marnie, but——"

"You're damn right it does!"

"Okay, so I had a party," he shouted back. "And according to your rigid morals, it got a little out of hand."

"'Morals' is another word you don't know the meaning of. And I'd classify smoking dope, drunkenness, topless girls, and flagrant marital infidelity as more than a 'little out of hand.'"

"Smoking dope? Who was smoking dope?"

"Some ancient hippie with white hair."

"I don't even know an ancient hippie with white hair."

"Then he must have been invited by someone else or just wandered in. All I know is, he wasn't a figment of my imagination."

"I don't know anything about any dope."

"All right, forget that. The rest of it is bad enough. I don't want David to be around Neanderthals who make disgusting references to women the way your friend—"

"That pilot is not a friend. I didn't even meet him until this afternoon, for crissake. We played chase."

"In test planes?"

"Yeah, so?"

"Aerobatics? Dangerous stuff, right?"

He shifted uneasily. "I'm a pilot. I fly."

"You take chances, Law," she cried. "The summer I met you, your challenge was to master a surfboard. You took so many risks on that damned thing, I couldn't bear to watch. And you're still taking risks, every time you stage dogfights in a jet bomber, and on the freeway every time you drive. You're little more than a well-trained daredevil."

"Damn you!" He came out of his chair so fast, Venus scuttled out of the way and cowered against the wall. "I'm not only a pilot, but a scientist."

"You still have no sense of your own mortality. You cross every threshold of danger that presents itself and go looking for the next one."

"What has any of this got to do with my wanting to spend time with my son?"

"I don't want David to fall in love with you and then be heartbroken when you fly off in a jet to play one-upmanship with your buddies and don't come back. I don't want him to lose you like—"

"Like what?"

She drew in a shuddering breath and hastily amended what she'd been about to blurt out. *Like I did.* "David is a sensitive young man who has a promising future. Fatherhood is just your newest challenge."

"You're wrong," he said stiffly.

"You might have a good time with him until the novelty wears off, but you'd soon be looking for a new toy and a new playmate. And where would that leave David?"

She aimed a finger at the center of his chest. "And if you think I'd let my son stay under the roof of this house after all that I saw going on here tonight, you've got another think coming, Colonel Kincaid. You don't even know how to feed your dog properly, much less a growing boy. And that brute killed one of your prettiest fish!"

She almost made it to the glass door before he caught up

with her. Catching both her upper arms, he drew her close against him. "Who did you love and lose, Marnie?"

"What?" she asked breathlessly.

"Who did you love and lose?"

"I don't know what you're talking about."

"Yes you do. Somebody broke your heart. Some man. Isn't that why you're so afraid to go with your feelings? Did some lost love make you shy of all other human relationships?"

Afraid that he might read the truth in her eyes, she wrenched her arms free and backed away from him. "What would you know about human relationships?"

"Admittedly not much," he said. "But I intend to learn. Soon. And with someone you keep referring to as 'your son,' but who, in fact, is *mine*."

With that statement the battle lines were drawn. His words struck terror in Marnie's heart, but she didn't let him see that. With her head held high, she left him standing in the rubble of his kitchen.

11

Through the rearview mirror of the Porsche he saw her car approaching. He slid from behind the wheel and met her in the driveway as she got out of her car. Behind a pair of sunglasses, her unsmiling face looked small and pale. He felt a compulsion to place his arms around her.

He didn't. Nearly every time he saw her, she plucked a protective chord in him. He should know by now, especially after she'd had the guts to crash that bacchanal last night, that the lady's temerity was disparate with her size.

"What do you want, Law?"

"Whatever happened to hi?" Stony silence. "I've been waiting over half an hour for you to get home. Doesn't that rate a hello?"

"What do you want?"

So much for the friendly approach. Maybe sincerity would work. "For us to be friends. Got a peace pipe?"

"Not funny."

He gnawed the corner of his lips with annoyance, knowing that to lose his temper now would be deadly to the purpose behind this surprise visit. The last thing he wanted was an argument.

She must not have glands, he thought nastily. That would explain why none of the tactics he used so successfully with other women worked on Marnie.

"Need help carrying that stuff in?" The backseat of her car was loaded with sacks of groceries and art supplies.

She mulled it over before giving in grudgingly. "As long as you're here, I could use an extra set of hands. Apparently there are no time clocks at the space center," she said as they took the path around to the back door.

"They're still working on that simulator. I told my superiors I had some personal business to take care of. Where's your key?"

He propped one sack of groceries on his knee while he opened the door. She preceded him inside. "Set them there on the table. I'll unload them later."

"We'll unload them now. Otherwise your ice cream will melt," he said, removing his sunglasses to peer into one of the sacks. "Swiss almond? My favorite."

"David's—" When she caught herself in a smile, she inverted it and turned her back to him. "David's too."

She disappeared into the back work area and deposited the art supplies. By the time she returned to the kitchen, he'd unloaded several bags and stacked their contents on the countertop.

"Law, I'll do that later."

He was determined not to let her get under his skin today. Calmly he held up a plastic bottle of mouthwash. "Where to?"

"Upstairs," she said on a sigh of surrender. "Put everything that goes upstairs here." She tapped a corner of the counter.

"Fine."

They worked in silence. Hers was hostile.

He continued to unload the sacks; she put the goods away in the various cabinets. He enjoyed watching her move with the grace and economy of motion that only the female of the species has in a kitchen. She bent and stretched, dipped and turned, opening doors and bumping drawers closed with her hip in a ballet he found enchanting.

The hem of her denim skirt bisected her kneecaps. When she bent over or stretched up on tiptoe to reach a shelf, he was treated to glimpses of smooth, bare thigh. She had on an oversized shirt with the tail knotted at her waist. Beneath that she had on a ribbed tank top. And beneath that he didn't think she had on anything. Just the thought of the soft cotton against her breasts made his sex feel warm and thick.

He nodded at the sodas she was placing in the refrigerator. "Can I have one of those?"

He knew he was pressing his luck. She hadn't warmed a single degree. She was still pissed about last night, he thought. She practically threw ice cubes into a glass before wrenching off the tab of the soda can and pouring him the drink. When she thrust it at him, the foam sloshed over his hand. He sucked it off. "Thanks."

Folding her arms over her middle, she faced him. "Now that the groceries are put away, now that you've got your drink, will you please state your business so I can get back to mine?"

He took a sip of his drink. Watching her closely, he said, "I called my lawyer this morning."

She said nothing, she didn't move, but her reaction was visible and drastic. Her eyes, which already looked wide and haunted, widened a bit more. What little color there was in her face faded. She wet her lips with her tongue, then clamped the lower one briefly between her teeth.

He wanted to touch her but didn't dare. He was afraid she would either start scratching and clawing or disintegrate. It looked like it could go either way.

"Sit down, Marnie. Let's talk about this reasonably," he suggested softly. "Please."

She nodded and distractedly lowered herself into the nearest chair at the dining table. If it had been a bed of nails, Law doubted she would have noticed. He remained standing and moved to the door. He stared out the window at the backyard and noticed the detached garage for the first time. There was a basketball hoop mounted on it above the driveway.

She'd provided David every advantage that had been within her means to provide. It seemed that fortune was either always smiling on someone or always frowning. Marnie was of the latter group. She had already had her share of heartache and didn't deserve any more. Law wished there were a painless way to do this. Unfortunately a sleepless night hadn't produced one.

"I asked my attorney what I'd have to do to get joint custody of David."

He heard a small sound, but when he turned around, her hand was covering her lips, which were rolled inward. "He told me it would be tough to do if you contested it, but not impossible. I'm hoping you won't contest it."

Her eyes were no longer haunted, but turbulent. "Don't you ever think of anyone but yourself, Law?"

He dropped his gaze to the toes of his shoes. "That's a fair shot, I guess. A little below the belt, though."

"I can't afford to be kind. Unless I fight you, and fight dirty, you'll ruin David's life."

He crossed the kitchen in one lunge and sat down across from her. "How could I ruin his life by becoming a part of it? A boy needs a father."

"He hasn't up till now."

"How do you know? Maybe he stopped wishing out loud for one because he was sensitive to your feelings."

He knew he had scored a point because she fell silent. "I know that what you saw last night makes me look bad, but I'd like to explain."

She didn't say anything, but raised her eyes to his. He tried not to let the silent reproach in them bother him. "I was mad about what happened here yesterday." It gratified him to see that the mention of that unsettled her. She shifted uneasily in her chair and nervously clasped her hands together. "I didn't want to stop, Marnie. I didn't want to be stopped. I wanted for it to go on until—"

"Law, don't."

"Until I was inside you, coming hard and fast."

She lurched out of her chair and headed for her back room. He followed her. When he got there, she was braced against her drawing board, clutching the edge of it and rocking slowly back and forth.

Hearing his footsteps, she spun around to confront him. "So in effect, that party was *my* fault?" she asked, pressing a hand against her chest.

"In effect." Vocally she scoffed at that. "Listen, will you?" he demanded, feeling the control on his temper slipping. "My frustration level was sky high. I felt like raising hell. I felt like getting a little drunk and, yes, getting laid before the evening was over.

"But after everybody got there I started looking around and thinking how superficial some of them were. For the most part they were hangers-on or jet jockeys playing a macho role. And then it occurred to me that I was the worst among them. My party mood evaporated before you ever got there. I wanted to be by myself so I could think about my priorities, but as you saw, there was little chance of that. I decided to ride out the party, make the most of it.

"Then you showed up, as daunting as a bad conscience.

When you asked me what I knew about relationships, it was like getting a bullet right between the eyes. I realized that I don't know much. I've never been required to know." He paused for effect. "I want to change that."

"You want to cut your teeth on David, use him as a guinea pig for this new you." She propped her hands on her hips. "Do you honestly think I'm stupid enough to fall for all this self-improvement tripe? You adore being Colonel Law Kincaid, NASA hero."

"All right, I'll admit it. Yes, I do. I've worked hard for it. I'm proud of what I did up there."

"So what are you going to say when people ask who David is? How are you going to introduce him?"

That was a question he'd asked himself repeatedly. Now he answered Marnie as honestly as he could. "I don't know yet. A lot will depend on David."

"David will never be given a chance to decide one way or the other. You make a pretty speech, Colonel, but you could never change. If I had guessed that you'd get it into your head to make David an active part of your life, I would have lied when you asked if he was your son."

"Who's really being selfish here, Marnie? I think you're afraid that if he gets to know me, he'll like me better than he likes you."

"That's not true! David loves me and knows how much I love him."

"Then whatever relationship develops between him and me couldn't possibly affect that, right?"

He'd trapped her, but it was a shallow victory and he drew little satisfaction from it. Probably because her fragile features seemed to shatter. Far from being vanquished, however, she stiffened her posture.

"Threaten all you want with lawyers. David is my son, legally and morally," she said, thumbing her chest with a laughably tiny fist. "I'll fight you with my last breath to keep him, Law."

"I hoped you would be reasonable. I should have known better."

"That's right. You should have. From now on consider me your enemy. Did you actually expect me to roll over and play dead when you're threatening the only important thing in my life?"

He strode across the room and backed her into the edge of the drafting table. Leaning over her, placing his face only inches above hers, he whispered, "I think that's what's really at issue here. Your life has no balance. David shouldn't be the only important thing in it."

"I didn't mean the *only* thing. There's my mother to take care of. I've got my work."

"What about yourself? Don't you deserve any consideration? What about fun? And sex?"

"Those are your priorities, not mine."

"They don't have to be priorities. I don't believe you've had *any* lately."

"What gives you that idea? Because I don't fawn over you, rub against you like a cat in heat and lick your ear?"

"Try it. You might like it."

"You're disgusting."

"Not disgusting, Marnie, normal. Oh, you've got the right equipment," he said, his eyes skating over her breasts. "It's all there and it all works. I've given it a test flight, remember?"

She tried to push him away and go around him. He angled her back against the table. "You won't open up and let your body fly full throttle. Why? Because some guy did a number on you that soured you on the rest of us?"

"Stop this."

"What did he do, Marnie, trade you for another girl, one who wasn't so uptight? Leave you stranded at the altar? Or couldn't he accept your devotion to David? What did he do that makes you freeze up every time a man touches you?"

Seeing that he had her speechless with rage, he pressed his advantage. "I believe, and I think any court in Texas would agree, that living with a father who enjoys life a little too much would be better for David than living with an old-maid aunt who's afraid to live at all."

He yanked her hard against him and kissed her lips angrily, then stormed out. When he reached his car, he leaned against the side of it and swore for a full sixty seconds. What was it about this woman that brought out the very worst in him?

12

Marnie felt like she'd been bludgeoned. She gripped her stomach and bent slightly at the waist as though in excruciating pain.

He couldn't take David away from her. He *couldn't*.

From a legal standpoint, he wouldn't have a leg to stand on. It was evident to anyone who looked at David that he was a healthy, well-adjusted youth. He'd never been neglected or mistreated either physically or emotionally. David would be the first to testify on her behalf, although the thought of placing him in a position to have to made her ill.

Surely Law would come to his senses and realize the advisability of leaving things as they were. He wouldn't put David through an ordeal like a custody dispute, would he? He was cocky and conceited, but he wasn't cruel.

Then again, a legal battle might not become necessary.

If David learned who Law was, he might choose to live with his father. There would be little she could do to prevent that. She would never forcibly exercise her custody rights at the sacrifice of David's happiness.

The most persistent and odious question that kept rearing its head was, did she owe it to David to tell him about Law?

She was so absorbed in thought that her telephone rang several times before she realized it. It was on the fifth ring before she picked it up.

"Hello? Oh, yes, Mr. Howard. How are you?"

"I'm fine. And you?"

"Fine."

"Miss Hibbs, the committee was most impressed with your proposal."

"Thank you. I'm glad to hear that." She waited for the other shoe to drop.

"However, we've elected to use someone else for the telephone directory."

"I see." A curtain of black seemed to have been drawn across her vision, blocking out all light, all hope.

"I can't emphasize enough how tough the decision was."

"I appreciate that."

"Maybe at some future date—"

"Thank you, Mr. Howard, for calling and letting me know. Good-bye."

She hung up, making the rejection of her work less

painful for both of them. She sat staring into near space for several minutes, then did something she rarely did. She burst into tears.

"Mom? Where are you?"

Her eyes were still red and puffy from hard crying when David came home. He arrived later than usual because he had gone to a friend's house after school. She was in the kitchen cooking dinner when he came through the door and dumped his books and gym bag into a chair.

"Hi."

"Hi." She injected a levity into her voice that she didn't feel, and overshot her mark. The gaiety sounded phony. "How was school?"

"I got ninety-eight on that history exam."

"Terrific. Use a glass, please," she said when he tipped the cold water pitcher in the refrigerator directly to his mouth, reminiscent of his father's habit of drinking straight from the container.

"It was worth a try." His disarming grin was another inherited trait. The grin vanished, however, the moment Marnie turned her head. "What's the matter, Mom?"

"Nothing."

"Have you been crying? Is it Grandma?"

"No. I spoke with her earlier today and she seemed groggy from medication but otherwise okay." She turned the meat in the skillet with a long fork. "Set the table please. Chicken fried steak tonight. It's almost ready. As soon as I make the gravy—"

"Mom, stop putting me off like I'm some dumb kid, okay?"

His irritation was justified. He hadn't seen her cry since they'd watched the news reports of the *Challenger* explosion. It didn't surprise her that he had noticed her tear-ravaged face and become upset in his own right.

He was no longer a child whose apprehensions could be dismissed without explanation. When something bothered her, it bothered him. It would frustrate, even panic her, if he shunned her concern over something that was worrying him.

Acknowledging that she was being unfair, she turned down the burner so the cutlets wouldn't overcook. "Mr. Howard called. I didn't get the telephone book commission."

"Damn!"

"That's what I said," she said with a twisted smile. "But that's that. Their decision was final and there's no sense mourning it. I'll have to work harder next time."

"They've got no taste!" he cried loyally. "You're the best."

"Thank you," she said, reaching out to stroke his cheek. "I'm glad to know I have your endorsement."

"Is something terrible going to happen? Does this mean we're going to be poor?"

"No, darling," she said, laughing softly. "Not any poorer than usual. It's just that I was planning to do something really special for your sixteenth birthday that I won't be able to do now."

"That's okay. Don't worry about that. You scared me. I thought it was something really awful."

She gave him a loving smile. "You're a great kid, you know that?" Fresh tears began to sting her eyes, so she turned back to the stove.

"Was Law here today?"

Marnie came around quickly.

David was seated at the table, twirling a pair of aviator sunglasses by the stem. Marnie hadn't noticed them.

Lying would be futile. Besides, she'd been lying to David frequently of late and didn't like it. "Yes, he, uh, stopped by."

"What for?"

"What for?" She shrugged and offered a feeble smile. "To say hi. He helped me carry in groceries from the car, drank a soda, and left. It wasn't a long visit by any means." She busied herself at the sink, washing lettuce. "What dressing do you want on your salad tonight?"

"Are you having an affair with him?"

"What?" This time she was nearly knocked off balance by the unexpected question. She didn't insult David with a glib reply. His expression was too serious to discard that easily.

She turned off the water faucet, dried her hands, and

removed the skillet of frying meat from the burner. Dinner could wait. Things like food had always taken second place to David's emotional needs.

"Of course I'm not having an affair with Law, David."

"It would be okay with me."

"I know. He told me what you said the other night before we went to that dinner together. Frankly it shocked me."

"I'm old enough to understand sex drives and all that. You and Law are grown-up, consenting adults."

"I appreciate your open-mindedness on the subject of my sexuality, but it's not at issue here. Law and I are not lovers."

"Then are you friends?"

"Not even what I'd call friends. We're merely acquaintances."

"Then how come he's dropping by in the middle of the day? Why are you going out on mysterious errands at night all of a sudden? You've never done that before. And every time we're around him, the two of you look at each other funny. You're so . . . keyed up, like you're afraid you'll say something wrong."

"I guess I'm nervous around him because he's a celebrity."

"You've never been nervous around anybody else."

"He's the first celebrity I've ever met." The words rang so hollow, she didn't blame David for his skeptical expression.

"Where'd you get the hickey?"

"What?" she asked, automatically raising a guilty hand to the faint mark on her neck. "That's an insect bite."

"It's a hickey, Mom," he repeated impatiently.

Marnie guiltily lowered her gaze. "All right, he kissed me. But that's as far as it's gone, David."

"I'm not mad about it. I told you it was okay. I just want you to level with me."

"And now I have." He peered deeply into her eyes and tapped out a rapid cadence on the surface of the table. She knew he wasn't ready to let the subject drop. "What else, David? There's something on your mind."

He fidgeted. He cleared his throat. He scratched his head. "Is Law . . . is he . . . you know, my dad?"

A tidal wave of astonishment and regret washed over her. It didn't knock her off her feet, but almost. Swaying slightly, she closed her eyes and blindly gripped the back of a chair.

"He is, isn't he?"

When she opened her eyes, David was still giving her a penetrating stare. She went around the chair she was holding on to for support and lowered herself into it carefully, as though if she moved too quickly she might unravel.

She gazed at the boy, now on the brink of manhood, whom she had cared for and loved since he was carried out of the hospital delivery room.

Episodes in his life flashed through her mind as clearly as the photographs in the picture albums. In seconds, her memory chronicled their life together, the times they had laughed and the times they'd been sad, the times they'd acted silly and the times they'd seriously pondered life's mysteries, the times they'd hugged and the very few times they'd been mad at each other.

He'd had to be consoled after seeing *Bambi* and scolded for giggling in church when his chewing gum accidentally fell into the offering plate. She recalled the smothering panic she'd experienced the first time he'd left for a week at Boy Scout camp and the enormous pride that had inundated her when he was named most outstanding boy at his junior high school graduation.

Perhaps she could claim a small portion of credit for the person he'd become. But the real credit overwhelmingly belonged to another: a tall, blond, athletic, naturally competitive overachiever.

"Yes, David. Law Kincaid is your father."

He let go a long, heavy exhalation, indicative of how tense he had been. He allowed himself several moments to absorb the truth before he spoke again. "Are you my mom? My real mom, I mean."

"No," she said, shaking her head gently. "I'm only fifteen years older than you, remember?"

"One of the girls in my class got pregnant last year."

"Well, I didn't. Law . . ." She paused to swallow, which she did with some difficulty. "Law picked Sharon over me. She was older, more mature. In his eyes I was still a child."

"Tell me about it."

"You know almost everything. Sharon got pregnant with you in the summer. We met Law on the beach." She summarized the events that had occurred in Galveston almost seventeen years earlier.

When she finished, David asked, "What made him suddenly want to see me after all this time?"

Noting the defensive hostility mounting in his eyes, she reached across the table and pressed his hand between hers. "Law never knew about you. Never, David. You must believe that. He didn't even remember your mother until recently." Quickly she told him about the letters.

"Grandma told him?"

"Yes."

"Why?"

"I found out only yesterday that she had sent the letters. I haven't had a chance to speak with her about it. It's water under the bridge, though, isn't it? Law found out about you. That's what's important."

"Why didn't you ever tell him, Mom?"

She pulled back and took a deep breath. "So many reasons, David. He had his own life. We had ours. I didn't see an easy way for them to integrate." She looked at him closely. "Do you blame me for not contacting him? Do you wish I had?"

"Well, kinda, yeah."

His truthful answer caused discomfort. He shifted restlessly in his chair. It caused Marnie's heart to ache.

"I have to take full responsibility for my decision," she

told him. "Grandma guessed that Law was your father, but I was the only one besides Sharon who knew."

Her eyes appealed to him for understanding. "He was a bachelor. He had an awesome future. I was intimidated by him. Most of all, I was afraid that he'd reject you, David."

"Has he?"

Though his voice had changed the year before, he suddenly sounded very young and vulnerable. Marnie's heart went out to him. "Can't you tell?"

His lips twitched at the corners before they fashioned a full-fledged smile. "I think he likes me. A little bit anyway."

"He likes you an awful lot."

He left his chair and began to roam aimlessly around the kitchen, touching objects that were familiar to him as though he'd never seen them before.

"I can't believe it. I always wondered who my dad was, but . . . *Law Kincaid*. Jeez," he whispered, raking his hand through his hair, "I—I . . . it's just too cool to believe." He grinned at her sheepishly. "Wait until the kids at school find out. The other day after the soccer game everybody was saying that we look alike. Do you think he and I look alike, Mom?" He waited anxiously for her answer and beamed a huge smile when she said, "The spittin' image."

"Can I call him? Can I tell him I know?"

"I—"

"Please? You were going to tell me anyway, weren't you? Or he was, wasn't he?"

"I suppose eventually, but—"

"Then I'm going to call him right now and let him know that he doesn't have to tell me. I already figured it out. Okay, Mom? Okay?"

Things were slipping away from her too quickly. She couldn't grip the lifeline. It was escaping her and there was nothing she could do about it. But David was looking at her with such animation and excitement, she didn't have the heart to refuse him.

"I guess that would be okay."

He whooped and lunged for the telephone. "What's his number?"

"I don't know. You'll have to look it up."

His smile deflated. "I'll bet it's unlisted." He attacked the telephone directory. "There's a Lawrence Joshua Kincaid."

"That's him."

"Joshua's my middle name too."

She nodded, afraid her voice would crack if she tried to speak. When it came time to name the infant, her parents had selected *David*. Sharon was indifferent. Marnie had remembered Law's full name and had given the newborn at least that much of his father's identity.

Law hadn't noticed the name on the hospital certificate when he saw it in the album. Marnie hadn't pointed it out to him because the fact that David bore his name seemed to seal his authority over his son's future.

"Hi, uh, Law," David was saying into the telephone,

"this is David. You know, David Hibbs?" There was a brief pause. "No, she's fine. She's standing right here. He says hi," he said to Marnie.

"Tell him I said hi."

"She says hi too. The reason I called is, uh, see . . ." He was shifting awkwardly from one foot to the other and stammering, both of which were uncommon to him. "I know that you're . . . that you and my mother . . . not my mom now, but Sharon . . . that you and she . . ."

He listened for a moment, then a smile as glorious and innocent as the first sunrise broke across his face. "Yeah. I figured it out. Hi, Dad!"

13

In under half an hour Law was at their front door.

During that time Marnie had fed the half-cooked dinner to the garbage disposal. David went upstairs to shower and change. Even so, he was standing at the front door, pacing, waiting for the sound of an approaching car long before Law's sporty Land Rover pulled up to the curb.

"He's here!" he shouted over his shoulder before barreling through the doorway.

From the living room window Marnie watched Law jog around the hood of his car. The two hastened toward each other, stopped, hesitated, solemnly shook hands, then seconds later embraced each other tightly.

Marnie's eyes smarted with tears, but she checked them. She was overjoyed for David that Law had the character to regard his son as a blessing instead of a consequence. But seeing them approach the house, their arms around each other's shoulders, made her physically ill with anxiety.

She was the picture of composure, however, when they joined her in the living room. "Thank you for letting me come over on such short notice," Law said politely.

"I don't think David would have allowed me to say no."

"I'm just glad you didn't already have plans," the boy said.

There was an awkward momentary lull in the conversation. Eventually Law and David looked at each other and began to laugh spontaneously, their joy bubbling over. Law clapped his hands together once and rubbed them together vigorously. "So are we all ready for dinner?"

"You bet, I'm starved," David said, turning toward the entrance.

"Marnie?"

Law's voice was soft, inquiring, sensitive to what he knew she must be feeling. She loved him for not being a heel, and resented him for the same reason. Dealing with a heel would have been easier than dealing with a man you loved who was trying to rob you of your life's focus.

"I'm bowing out tonight."

"What? Why? Didn't David tell you the invitation to dinner was meant for both of you? I thought I'd made that clear."

"You did. It was generous of you to include me, but I think you and David should have this evening alone."

"I think the three of us need this evening alone," he argued quietly.

"Hey, what's going on?" David said, poking his head around the door. "What's keeping you?"

"I'm not going."

"Why not, Mom? Why don't you want to come?" It seemed inconceivable to him that anyone would pass up having dinner with Law.

"I'm very tired."

"Is it because of the phone book thing?" David asked, coming back into the room.

"What about it?" Law wanted to know.

"Nothing."

"She didn't get the job."

They had answered in unison, but David's statement was the one Law heard. He looked at Marnie quickly, then down at the floor, then back at her. "I'm sorry. I know you were counting on that."

"Not *counting* on it," she said defensively. "It would have been a nice commission to get. The exposure, the honor, and all that. But *c'est la vie*," she said with a phony smile.

"You were one of the final three," David said, trying to be encouraging. "That's really good."

But not best. And anything other than first didn't count. For David's benefit, though, she smiled. "I'm going to repeat that to myself a thousand times while you two are at dinner. Have a nice evening."

"Sure you won't come, Mom?".

"I'm sure. Run along. If Law made reservations, you shouldn't be late."

"Here, David," Law said, tossing him a set of car keys, "start the car."

"You bet!" David caught the keys and raced for the front door.

Law hadn't taken his eyes off Marnie. She felt distinctly uncomfortable beneath that hot blue gaze as he crossed the room toward her. "Are you upset?"

"Over the contract I didn't get? No."

"That's crap, Marnie. You're upset. Don't keep that anger locked inside. Let it go. Raise hell. Scream and thrash your limbs. Pitch a fit. Throw a tantrum. Don't be so damn gracious about losing out on a good commission."

"What good would a tantrum do?"

"Absolutely none, but you might feel better."

"I wouldn't. I'd feel ridiculous."

"At least the rest of us slobs would know that you're human, that you've got feelings." He moved a step nearer and brushed his thumb across her cheekbone. "But I know you've got feelings. They show in your eyes. And right now you look like I would have if I'd got sucked into a black hole while I was in space. I've never seen eyes look so bleak. Is it because David found out about me?"

She nodded, wishing she could yield to the temptation to rest her cheek in his palm. One quarter turn of her head and she could. But she didn't. She wouldn't allow herself even that much intimacy with him. Instead, she angled her head away from his touch.

"His finding out was inevitable," she said. "I've known that since you first came here. He's too smart, too perceptive." She drew in a shaky breath. "Anyway, now it's done and I don't have to dread it anymore."

"You look on it as a tragedy? David doesn't."

"He's ecstatic," she said on a bitter laugh. "What boy wouldn't be thrilled to discover that his father is a national hero?"

"Oh, I see. It's not necessarily me he's happy about. It could have been anybody famous."

"Law, don't." She moaned. "Don't pick a fight with me. I'm too exhausted to battle with you tonight."

"How'd he find out?"

"He guessed. He noticed your sunglasses here and asked me why you'd come by in the middle of the day." She looked away. "He jumped to the conclusion that we were having an affair."

"What did you tell him?"

"I told him no!"

"I mean about how he was conceived."

"Everything. He had also jumped to the wrong conclusion that I was his birth mother."

He touched her again, this time sliding his fingers around the back of her neck, encircling it, "You are his mother. I won't forget that. David certainly won't. Right now he's excited about me. But that doesn't diminish his love for you."

He moved closer still, until she could feel his breath on her face. "This is a family occasion. Let's celebrate it together. Come to dinner with us."

For the span of several seconds she was mesmerized by his eyes and persuasive tone of voice. Then she shook her head. "No, Law. Out of almost sixteen years, I think you and David deserve this time alone together."

"Did anybody ever tell you you're stubborn?"

"Just about everyone I've ever met."

Smiling ironically, he dropped his hand. "Okay, but we won't be gone long."

"Take your time."

She saw him to the door. David waved at her from the driver's seat of the Land Rover. "Hurry up, Dad, I'm starved," he called with the ease of lifetime practice.

Marnie closed the front door and leaned against it. The pain in her throat from having held back tears was almost unbearable. It was a profound relief to submit to it. Her sobs shook her petite body. Tears streamed down her face. She groped her way back into the living room and collapsed into one of the easy chairs . . . the one in which she had almost made love with Law.

She lost track of time while sitting curled in the chair, sobbing. Eventually the hard weeping subsided. She went upstairs and washed her face in cold water. The pipes were creaky, reminding her of the advice given her the last time the plumber had been called. He had recommended that she replace all the plumbing.

The house was old and becoming rundown. She'd made it as attractive as her budget would allow, but it was certainly no match for Law's decorator-perfect house. It had no swimming pool, no aquarium built into the wall, no friendly dog awaiting the master's return.

Marnie left the bathroom and went down the hall to David's bedroom. She paused outside the door for a long time. Finally she went in, noticing the dirty clothes he'd stepped out of before his shower. They were lying in an untidy heap on the floor.

Starting with them, she began collecting items and articles of clothing and setting them on his bed. She hoped she had time to finish before they returned.

"Why do you think she did it?" David asked his father several hours later as they pulled away from the curb.

Law was driving, but his eyes were on the rearview mirror, where he could see Marnie standing in the open doorway, a tiny silhouette, looking like she was about to be swallowed by the house.

"I guess for the reason she said," Law replied. "She felt like we needed time together." He glanced at David across the console. "Does the idea of living with me for a while appeal to you?"

"Yeah, sure," David answered, his hearty approval evident in his sparkling eyes. "I think it's going to be really great." Gradually his smile faded. "I just keep thinking about Mom staying by herself. 'Course it's only for a little while. I don't want you to think you're stuck with me forever," he rushed to add.

"You're welcome for as long as you want to stay, David. I mean that."

The smile David gave him tugged at his heart. The guys at the center would hoot if they knew that several times during the course of the evening, the cocksure Law Kincaid had had to combat tears or risk making a public spectacle of himself.

He and David had spent several hours over an enjoyable dinner. The better he got to know his son, the better he liked him and the prouder he became that his seed had produced such an outstanding young man. He had wanted to announce to everybody, "Hey, this is my son."

David was friendly, mannerly, and knew how to conduct himself properly. For his deportment, Marnie deserved an award. She had done exceptionally well in rearing a child alone. These days two parents were rarely so successful, Law mused. He knew that from listening to some of the horror stories his colleagues told about their kids.

"If only she hadn't looked so sad when we left," David said now, bringing Law's attention back to him. "But it was her idea for me to stay with you. She had everything packed when we got there."

They had almost stumbled over the suitcases in the hall-way when they came through the front door after dinner. "Who's going somewhere?" David had asked, thinking he was making a joke.

In all seriousness, Marnie had told them that she thought it would be a good idea for David to move in with Law for a while. At first they'd been too stunned to speak. But after trying the idea on for size, they realized they liked it very much and had readily agreed with her.

"Do you think she really meant it when she said she didn't mind, that she wanted me to?" David asked uncertainly.

"We can only take her word for it, David. She repeated it several times." Law sounded far more confident than he felt. Marnie looked on the verge of emotional collapse when she hugged David good-bye, though she'd put up a brave front.

"She knows it's just temporary, right?"

"Right," Law answered.

"She knows I'll be home on my birthday. I promised."

"A promise we'll both keep."

"Then I guess she's okay with it."

"I guess so." Marnie had seemed anything but okay when they'd left. But she'd been emphatic about David leaving right away. Tonight. It was as though she didn't want time in which to reconsider.

Law admitted to himself that he was delighted with the arrangement. Obviously so was David. Then why did each feel that he was, to some extent, deserting Marnie?

Venus went berserk over seeing David again. She chased her own tail in tight, mad circles before she eventually got winded and calmed down.

"Can I go swimming?" David asked almost as soon as he'd deposited his suitcases in one of the empty guest rooms.

"Be my guest. But here are the rules of the house. No wet towels or clothing left on the deck. Hang them in the laundry room."

"Just like at home."

"And make sure the gate is locked and that you turn off the pool light when you come in."

"Yes, sir."

It was almost an hour later before David walked into the small den Law used as an office at home. The walls were covered with framed photographs of him as a navy jet pilot taken aboard aircraft carriers and at air bases all over the world. Others documented his career as an astronaut. Noticing a picture of the *Victory* space shuttle's launch, David remarked on it.

"Mom woke me up early that morning to watch the blastoff. I was almost afraid to after seeing the *Challenger*. We cheered when everything went all right."

"So did I," Law said with a self-deprecating smile. "I'll get you one of those pictures for your room tomorrow and have all the crewmen sign it."

"Thanks. That'd be cool."

"Did Venus come in when you did?"

"Yeah."

"I haven't seen her. She's usually trying to climb into my lap this time of the night."

"She's, uh, in my bed."

Law threw up his hands. "Women!"

David laughed, but it was almost forced. "I guess you've been with lots of them."

"What, women?"

David cleared his throat. "Yeah."

Law tried to catch his eye, but David wouldn't look directly at him. "Is there something you want to ask me about, David?"

He shrugged, his bony shoulders bobbing first up then down. "Mom and I have talks about it. Sex, I mean."

"And?"

"Well, I'm no kid. I know all about it."

"Hmm."

"I haven't gone all the way yet, but, of course, I've been French-kissing for years."

Law tried to keep his face impassive. Leaning back in his cream leather chair, he linked his hands over his flat stomach and said, "Of course."

"And there are some girls who'll let you, you know, kinda touch them . . . in places."

"Hmm."

"Mom's not stupid. She said she knew that I'd want to, you know . . . sleep with girls."

"Yes."

"She said it would be unnatural if I didn't. Jeez!" He groaned. "I sound like a real jerk."

"Most of us do when we talk about this subject, David. Forget about how you sound. Just go on and say what's on your mind."

"Well, Mom said I shouldn't think of a woman just as a body, but I should also admire her mind and brain and stuff, you know, what makes her that person. That I should respect women and never do anything exploit . . . explo—"

"Exploitative?"

"Yeah, that. I know what it means, I just couldn't get it out."

"Your mother is right, David."

David fixed him with a stare identical to his own. "You didn't. Not with my mother."

Law was the first to look away from their long stare. Ordinarily he resented correction and would have reacted to it angrily. He was his own worst critic and rarely the recipient of criticism from someone else. It was even rarer that he had a guilty conscience. But beneath his son's scrutiny, he felt uneasy and guilty as hell.

"No, I didn't, David. I'm hoping that you'll behave more responsibly in your relationships than I did with Sharon."

"You're not mad at me for saying that, are you?"

"No. On the contrary, I respect you for pinning my ears to the wall about it. Your mother wasn't honest with me, but I should have taken it upon myself to ensure she didn't get pregnant."

"I don't even remember her, so I guess that's why I'm not really mad at you about it. If you had hurt my mom, Marnie, I mean, that'd be a different story." He flashed a fleeting grin. "Besides, if you'd used a condom, I wouldn't even be here."

"For that reason, and only that reason, I'm glad I didn't."

David ducked his head and muttered shyly, "Well, good night again."

"We'll have to leave early to get you to school on time."

"I'll be up. Mom packed my alarm clock."

He lingered beside the door, tracing the grain in the wood with his fingertip. "Is there something else, David?" Law asked, noticing his reluctance to leave. "Another rule of the house is that whoever has something on his mind speaks up."

"I was just wondering why you've been hanging around my mom lately. Was it because of me?"

"We've spent a lot of time talking about you," Law answered evasively.

"Oh," he said, looking crestfallen. "I thought it might have been because you think she's pretty."

"I do."

"You do?" David's face lit up.

"Very pretty."

"Ah, well, that's good, that's real good. I gotta go to bed now. Good night. It's great being here, Dad."

"Great having you."

For several minutes after David left the room, Law continued to smile. Each time he recalled a particular snatch of their conversation, he would smile again. He was surprised at himself for deriving so much satisfaction from their heart-to-heart discussion.

He turned out the light in the den and went into his own bedroom, undressed, and got into bed. Stacking his hands beneath his head, he stared at the ceiling fan that was slowly rotating overhead and thought about how unsatisfying other aspects of his life had been lately, namely his sex life.

Come to think of it, he hadn't had a sex life since meeting Marnie Hibbs again.

What had it been, one week, two? Law Kincaid going two weeks without getting laid? Outrageous! Unheard of! If word of it got around the office, he'd never hear the end of it.

Funny, though, he didn't feel inclined to do anything about it. He'd rather wait. He'd rather wait for her. His desire was so strong as to be painful at times, but at other times so sweet as to be a pleasure in and of itself.

The circling blades of the fan cast swirling shadows on the walls. The shadows were the exact gray color of Marnie's eyes. From her eyes, his thoughts wandered to her mouth, its seductive shape, its sweet taste, its involuntary, and even unwilling, passionate response to his kisses.

He thought about her breasts, small, but super-sensitive to his touch. And the taste of her skin. And how adorable her belly button was. And the sexy, catchy little sound she had made in her throat when his lips . . .

As he drifted off to sleep, his fantasies followed him into his dreams.

14

Marnie was so nervous, she nearly created a blob of the dot above the *i* in David's name. But she caught the drop of cake frosting just in time and ended up dotting the *i* perfectly. She wanted everything to be absolutely perfect for his birthday dinner.

"We can have the celebration at my house," Law had suggested several days earlier.

"No, I want him to be at home that night." Then, realizing Law's house was becoming more home to David than her address, she said, "I'd like to have his birthday dinner here."

"Fine." He had agreed with a smile. He went out of his way to be civil these days. "Anything I can do to help?"

"No, thank you," she had said, being equally civil. "It won't be a lavish party by any means. Only the three of us. But I want to cook his favorite foods and make it a super-special occasion. He's looked forward to it for so long."

Just then David had come bounding down the stairs, carting a box of belongings on his shoulder. His room in Marnie's house was gradually emptying while the one at Law's house continued to fill up. Marnie tried not to let that transference of his possessions panic her and kept reminding herself that teenagers liked to be surrounded by their own things. It made them feel independent.

"Ready, Dad?"

"If you are."

"We're going miniature golfing tonight," David had informed her.

"Have fun."

"Want to come?" Law had offered.

"Yeah, Mom, want to come? But I'd better warn you, Dad, she pouts if she doesn't win."

"I do no such thing!" She had swatted David playfully. "I'd like to come, but no thanks. I've got a piece that needs my attention tonight."

"Okay. 'Bye. See you tomorrow. Can I drive, Dad?"

"Sure," Law had said, pitching him the keys.

"Is he careful in that thing?" Marnie asked, glancing worriedly at the Porsche.

"Very. He's getting in a lot of driving practice. He'll pass that part of his test with flying colors."

"Only five more days. I'm not sure I'm ready to turn him loose on the roads."

"He's a very responsible driver, Marnie."

"I know. It's the other crazies I'm worried about."

That had been five days ago. Today was the big day. She was getting the cake-baking out of the way early so she would have the afternoon free to accompany David to the Department of Motor Vehicles after school for his driving test.

David had been anticipating this day for as long as he'd been a teenager. She was apprehensive about his driving alone but looked forward to sharing that rite of passage into adulthood with him.

The last two weeks had been the most difficult of her life, except for a few anxious ones seventeen years earlier, when she had been afraid that Sharon might abort Law's child despite her father's edict.

Since David had left, the old house was silent during the daytime and spooky at night. She woke up each time the wood settled and creaked.

She missed him terribly. His absence was as persistent and painful as a toothache. It was made even worse by not knowing when it would end. So far David hadn't mentioned coming home. The fear that he might never was about to kill her.

But she had made a decision the night he discovered that Law was his father. David would resent her for the rest of his life if she kept him separated from Law one day more. She'd nearly gone mad after watching him drive away with Law, leaving her alone. But deep down she knew she'd done the right thing.

They'd arranged it so that Law drove him to school every morning, which was far out of the way of the Johnson Space Center. He hadn't complained of the inconvenience. In the afternoons she picked David up from school. They spent an hour or so together before Law retrieved him on his way home.

She coveted those hours with David and hadn't let anything interfere with them, not her trips to the rest home to visit her mother, not her work. Losing the commission on the telephone directory had been a financial and professional setback. She'd been doubly disappointed because she wouldn't be able to carry out the surprise she had planned for David's birthday.

However, a few days after rejecting her for that job, Mr. Howard's agency had contacted her for another project. She had been flattered and thrilled. The work was progressing very well and the client was already discussing future commissions with her.

She tingled at the thought of David's surprise, which, thanks to the work she'd gotten, had been affordable after all. He was going to "have a cow," as he would say. It was gratifying to know she could do something special for him.

Competing with Law wasn't easy. He'd taken David flying with him several times, and David had loved it. David had even gone with him to Annapolis, where Law had delivered the commencement speech to the graduating cadets.

David, naturally, had stars in his eyes and was always brimming with enthusiasm for all the wonderful things his father had done for him. Marnie was delighted for him but couldn't help feeling jealous. Tonight *she* was going to put the stars in David's eyes.

By mid-afternoon she'd cleaned the house, decorated the dining room, and prepared dinner so that it was ready to go into the oven. She showered and dressed and, congratulating herself on her perfect planning, was on her way downstairs when the telephone rang.

"Hi, Mom."

"Hi, I'm on my way. Will you be out front or at the gym door?"

"I'm glad I caught you. Dad's already here. He's going to take me. We'll be over as soon as I'm finished."

Marnie's disappointment was so crushing, she couldn't speak.

"Mom? Are you there?"

"Cer-certainly. I'm just—"

"Busy. I know. Dad said you'd be tearing around trying to get things ready for tonight. If he takes me to get my license, that'll be a big help, right?"

"Right," she said dismally.

"Don't go to any special pains for dinner. It's only my birthday."

"I'll go to special pains if I want to, thank you very much." She wasn't going to let him know how disappointed she was. That would only spoil his day. "Be careful, David. Good luck. Do well. And I'll be standing by with a congratulatory soda when you get here."

"Okay, 'bye."

She hung up, feeling depression settling down on her like a suffocating blanket. She submitted to it only for a second, then by an act of will threw it off.

This was David's sixteenth birthday. Neither he nor Law could have known how much she'd looked forward to going with him to take his driver's test. They hadn't deliberately excluded her. It had been a thoughtful gesture, not a malicious one, for Law to volunteer to take him.

She still had last-minute things to do before they arrived. This disappointment wasn't going to keep her from giving David a beautiful birthday, one he would never forget.

"No wonder you're in such terrific shape," Law said to David as he pushed away his plate. "You've had meals like that all your life."

"I told you she was a good cook." David beamed a smile at Marnie before popping the last homemade roll into his mouth. "But you outdid yourself on the pot roast this time, Mom."

She basked in his praise. "I'm glad you enjoyed it. I only hope you left room for dessert."

"This corner right here." He pointed to a space between two ribs. It was a childhood game they used to play.

"Then I won't keep you waiting any longer. It'll be served as soon as I clear this away." She stood up and began stacking dishes onto a tray.

"I'll help." Law scooted his chair back.

"You don't have to."

"I know that."

"Well, it's my birthday, so I'm just going to sit here and see how loud I can belch."

"David Hibbs, you—"

"Only kidding, Mom."

She made a face at him and carted the tray into the kitchen.

"Where do these go?" Law asked, holding up a pair of crystal salt and pepper shakers.

"Last cabinet on the right. Second shelf."

"Great-looking table. Great dinner."

"Thank you."

"There's nothing so sensually stimulating as a good dinner complete with flowers, candlelight, and . . ." He moved up behind her and slid one hand around her. He cupped her breast and gave the delicate center an airy caress with his thumb. "A beautiful woman."

She sucked in a quick breath and turned in his arms. "Law! What are you doing?"

"Having more fun than I've had all day," he whispered around a wicked grin before settling his mouth warmly and possessively over hers. His hands slid over her derriere and pulled her against the front of his body.

"I've been nice. I've given you space. I've given you time. I haven't pushed. But, dammit, I've waited long enough. I want you, Marnie." He tilted his hips forward and watched her pupils dilate. "You want me too," he said roughly before giving her a long, languorous, delicious kiss.

"Law?" Several long, breathless minutes passed before she was able even to gasp his name.

"Hmm? God, you're gorgeous." His eyes scoured her face.

"Law?"

She was barely given an opportunity to weakly whimper his name before he treated them to another kiss, where each fervently but tenderly devoured the other's mouth.

At last he raised his head. "Our son is waiting," he said hoarsely. "We'll get back to this later." He gave her breast another little glancing blow with his thumb and felt the hard projection of her nipple. "The sooner the better. In the meantime, what can I help you with?"

He could start by supporting her, because she wasn't sure she could continue standing on her own. She managed, however, and soon the candles on the cake were lit and she was bearing it into the dining room, where David was waiting.

"You're not going to do anything corny like sing 'Happy Birthday,' are you?"

Marnie glanced up at Law and gave him an impish smile. Then the two of them broke into loud song. David sank low in his chair and poked his fingers in his ears. All three were laughing before the grand finale.

"Make a wish."

"Mom." David groaned, rolling his eyes. He complied, however, and blew out all the candles in one breath. Marnie sliced the three-layer chocolate cake she had worked so hard on and served them both monstrous pieces, which they voraciously eliminated in record time.

"Now it's time for presents." She left the room and returned with a gift-wrapped box. "Open this one first."

"First? You mean there's more than one?"

She gave him a mysterious smile and said in a singsong voice, "I'll never tell. You know how I feel about birthday surprises."

Barely able to contain her excitement, she stood behind David's chair as he unwrapped a new set of clothes.

"Cool, Mom!" he exclaimed, holding the pants and shirt up to him. "These are so cool."

"You like them?"

"Yeah, they're great."

They were so involved with their discussion of the clothes, which bore the latest status label, that they didn't notice when Law moved to the window and glanced out.

When he turned back into the room, he tipped his head toward the front yard. "You'll have to go outside to open my present," he told David.

"Outside?"

"Go on. You too, Marnie."

Law ushered them through the front door. David had taken only a few steps when he spied the shiny new sports car parked in the driveway. He came to an abrupt standstill.

Blue eyes bugging, mouth agape, he spun around. "Where'd it come from?"

"It was delivered. Right on time, thank goodness."

"You mean that's . . . that's . . . that's my present? An Iroc? An *Iroc*?"

"Happy birthday." Law dangled a set of car keys in front of David's nose.

David stared at the keys, at Law, at Marnie. Then he executed a back flip in the grass, grabbed the keys from Law, and raced toward the new car.

"Wait," Law said, laughing as he ran after him, "there are a few things I need to show you before you take off in it."

Law and David got into the car. Marnie slipped back into the house unnoticed. She was afraid that at any second she might start screaming, so she crammed a fist against her mouth to hold it in.

The gaiety of the birthday party table seemed to mock her. Quickly, angrily, she blew out the candles in the centerpiece. The new set of clothes she'd given David were lying forgotten among the tissue paper she had lovingly wrapped them in. They, too, seemed to be laughing at her. With a wide, angry swipe of her hand, she swept them off the table and onto the floor.

She took another gift-wrapped box out of her skirt pocket and tried to destroy it, raking at the paper and ribbon with her nails.

"He said to tell you he's gone to show his car to Jack but

won't be long," Law said, breezing into the house. "You didn't say much—" He pulled up short when she whirled around, confronting him with the disposition of a cobra about to strike.

"What should I have said, Law? What? That no, he couldn't accept the car? That it's too expensive and flashy a car for a high school boy who only got his license today? That you should have consulted me first? That it wasn't your place to give him something on that grand a scale? Which of these things should I have said to burst David's bubble?"

He said nothing for several moments. Then, "It never occurred to me to consult you."

"Well, it should have. I'm his mother."

"And I'm his father."

"You're Santa Claus!" she shouted.

Tears were streaming down her flushed cheeks, but she didn't even notice. Nor did she realize that she was holding her arms straight down at her sides, her small body rigid with fury.

"You came into David's life bearing gifts. You're larger than life, magnificent, like some god. Parenting is easy when you're not the one who changes diapers or stays up all night with a kid's earaches. You never had to discipline him while your heart was breaking for having to. No, you missed all that, didn't you?"

"You chose to rear David."

"And I'd choose to again. I love him. I would have fed

him from my own breasts if I'd had milk. I've made thousands of sacrifices to give him a quality life."

She held up a hand to stave off the comments she could see rising to his lips. "Everything I've done, I've done gladly. I neither want nor expect his gratitude. I know I have his love. I just want *you* to understand how much I resent your coming into his life now and trying to lure him away from me."

"I'm not, Marnie."

"You already have. He's living with you, not me. You gave him a young man's fantasy car and I gave him—"

She broke off and turned her back to him, clutching the small box between her hands.

"What?"

"Just go. Wait for David outside. I don't want you here. I'm furious with you for undermining me."

"What's in that box? Another present?"

"Go, Law." He reached around her and snatched the box out of her hands. "Give me that." She lunged for it, but he held it over his head, way beyond her reach. He opened the box. A set of ignition keys dropped into his hand.

"A car." Swearing savagely, he closed his eyes and dug into the sockets with his thumb and middle finger.

She rubbed tears off her cheeks and faced him defiantly. "A *used* car. Not new, not flashy, not cool. Just dependable transportation. He would have been doing back flips over it if you hadn't bought him that four-speed, rolling stereo!" She made a disparaging gesture toward the driveway.

"Marnie, I'm—"

"No!" she said harshly, backing away from his touch. "I don't want your apology or your pity. I don't want anything from you. I never did. I can't deny David the advantages you're able to give him, but I won't take anything from you personally."

"I never meant to interfere. It certainly wasn't my intention to hurt you."

"Well, despite your good intentions, that's exactly what you've done, Law. Now just please leave." She could feel her control slipping. To contain it, she wrapped her arms around her waist. "I don't want you to come here again. David may choose to live with you permanently. If he does, he and I will work out times to be together, but I don't want to see you anymore."

She aimed a finger at the center of his chest. "Never, *never*, tell him about the car I bought for him. It would only make him feel terrible and lay a guilt trip on him."

Bending at the waist, she picked up the set of new clothes and carefully refolded them. "Here, he might want to wear these before I see him again." She passed them to Law.

She ran upstairs and barely got her bedroom door shut behind her before she succumbed to a torrent of tears.

The following morning when she entered the kitchen to brew coffee, she was surprised to find that it was spotlessly clean. The dining room, too, had been cleared of all evidence of the birthday dinner, though the floral centerpiece was still on the table. Apparently Law and David had cleaned up before they left.

Sipping her coffee, she wondered how she should go about selling the car she'd just bought. Perhaps the dealership would take it back and give her a refund. While brooding on the unlikelihood of that, her telephone rang.

"Miss Hibbs?"

"Yes."

The caller identified himself as one of the doctors on staff at the rest home. "Your mother suffered a severe stroke a few minutes ago. She's being transported by ambulance to the hospital now."

15

It was twilight when she turned onto Law's street. She parked in front of his house and for a moment just sat behind her steering wheel, too tired and dispirited to move.

Finally she garnered enough energy to push open the car door and walk to the front door. She heard the doorbell peal and Venus's suspicious growl before Law opened the door. All he had on was a wet swimsuit. He seemed shocked to see her.

"Hello, Law. Is David here?"

"No."

"Oh." She hadn't thought beyond driving here and seeing David.

"Come in."

It took less energy to do as he said than it did to think of an alternative. She stepped inside and he closed the door. Venus regarded her closely, then moved forward to nuzzle her knee. Automatically she reached down and patted the animal's head.

"Beats all I've ever seen," Law commented, running his hand through his wet hair. "Even though Labs are characteristically docile, Venus nearly eats alive every other female."

"She realizes I'm no threat." Then, without giving him any warning, she said, "My mother died this afternoon."

Law's smile collapsed. He lowered his hand to his side. She watched him swallow. He glanced away, then back. "I'm sorry, Marnie. What happened?"

"She had another stroke this morning. The worst yet. I arrived at the hospital just a few minutes after she was brought in. I was with her all day in the ICU."

"All day? Alone? Why didn't you call us?"

"There was no reason to. She never regained consciousness."

"But you were conscious and shouldn't have endured that by yourself."

She shook her head. "The hospital would have made David uneasy. He couldn't say good-bye to Mother, so his being there would have been obligatory and pointless. It was best this way. She had a very peaceful death. I guess that's the most any of us can hope for. Although," she said, finding it more difficult to speak, "she died an unhappy woman."

"Marnie."

Law reached for her, taking her narrow shoulders between his strong hands. She resisted, but he stubbornly held on, refusing to let go. Finally Marnie surrendered and let herself be pulled against him.

She rested her cheek on his bare damp chest. He plowed the fingers of one hand into her hair. His other moved consolingly up and down her back.

"I'm sorry, Law. So sorry."

"Sorry?" He let her cry quietly for several minutes, then whispered, "Tell me about it."

She sniffed noisily. He'd got her front all wet. His swim trunks had left a large dark patch of wetness on the front of her skirt, but she didn't even notice.

"One day this week while I was visiting her, I asked why she'd sent you those letters."

"Did she try to deny it?"

"No. As you guessed, she had wanted to get caught. That's why she put my return address on the envelopes. She said she knew you would track us down."

"How did she know I was David's father?"

"She suspected it all along and said that she would have to be stupid not to know. Mathematically your affair with Sharon fit with the date of David's birth. Then the older David got, the more he grew to look like you."

Marnie raised her head and looked up at him. "Law, she didn't send you those letters on David's behalf. She wasn't thinking about him at all. She was being spiteful."

"You don't owe me an apology for her, Marnie."

"I feel like I do. The more we talked the more vindictive she became. She asked me why you should be allowed to go on living a charmed life when her whole family had been broken apart because of you."

She tipped her head forward, resting her forehead on his sternum. "Mother seems to have forgotten Sharon's rebelliousness and deviousness. I saw no point in arguing with her. Besides, I was afraid to. The doctor had warned me that her blood pressure was high."

"I'm certain you handled it the best way possible. And for the record, my life has been much more charmed since David entered it." He set his chin on the crown of her head. "Did you tell her that he was spending time with me?"

"Yes, and she laughed maliciously. She wanted to believe that he would be an inconvenience to you. A liability." She tilted her head up. "I'm sorry for any mental anguish you suffered because of those letters, Law."

"Not anguish. Annoyance, maybe. And it was temporary. Don't worry about it anymore, Marnie. It's over. We can all be glad."

It felt good to be held in his arms, to have his hands loosely propped on each side of her waist. Because it felt so good, she forced herself to step out of his embrace.

"Where is David? Will he be back soon? I need to tell him about his grandmother."

"He went to an all-nighter at a friend's house. Don't worry," he said when he noticed her concern, "I called the boy's parents before giving my consent. The Moores."

"Oh, Jack Moore. He and David have been good friends for ages. Nice family."

"I concluded that and let him go on the condition that once he got there he stay until morning. I didn't want him cruising on a Saturday night."

"I agree. Well, I guess I can find him at the Moores, then. Good-bye, Law. Thank you for letting me cry on your . . ." Rather than say the word *chest*, she finished on a lame smile and turned toward the door.

"Whoa, whoa." He caught her arm and brought her around. "May I offer a suggestion?" She cocked her head inquisitively. "Why don't you let David enjoy his party? There's nothing to be done tonight, is there?"

"No. The arrangements have already been made."

"Then tomorrow morning's early enough for David to get the sad news. This is an end-of-school bash. All the Pepsi, pizza, and *Playboy* they can handle, he told me."

"Well . . ." She combed her fingers through her hair several times. "I guess you're right. Why spoil his night? Give me a call in the morning when he gets home and I'll come back then."

She reached for the doorknob. Law bracketed her shoulders with his hands again.

"May I make another suggestion?" Again she gave him an inquiring look. "Stay here tonight."

Her mouth dropped open. "What?"

"Considering your emotional state, you'd be a menace on the freeway. Besides that, I doubt you've got the stamina to drag yourself to your car. And regardless of your physical limitations, I don't think you should be alone tonight."

"I'll manage."

"But why should you merely manage? I've got several bedrooms that have never been slept in."

"Although the beds have certainly been used."

He winced. "Don't you ever forget anything? I promise that no half-clad couples will bother you tonight. My friends all know that I've got a teenager living here now and that that kind of behavior is taboo."

"What'd you tell them?"

"That they'd have to find someplace else."

"I mean about David."

"I haven't told them anything."

"Because you don't want the scandal."

"Because I don't owe anybody an explanation for an erection I had seventeen years ago!" He reigned in his temper and continued more calmly. "Explaining him means explaining you, the lady he calls mom. Explaining you gets too damn complicated. So I've let people draw their own conclusions."

"And?"

He gave an eloquent shrug. "I don't know. Nobody's dared voice an opinion on where he sprang from. But he's got everybody eating out of his hand. He's gone with me to the center several times. I'm amazed by how much he knows about the space program."

"He's been interested in it all his life."

"An interest which you cultivated. Thanks." He encircled her wrist with his strong fingers and gave it a slight yank. "Now, are you going to come peacefully?"

"I'm not going to come at all."

His lips twitched, heralding a naughty smile. "Ever?"

She spun around and reached for the doorknob again.

"Okay, okay, sorry. Poor joke and even poorer timing. See, in the astronaut office, when we're not jabbering about flying, we're jabbering about sex. That's why these little double entendres just naturally pop out sometimes." He closed his fingers tighter around her wrist. "Nearest shower is this way."

"Law, I can't," she protested as she stumbled along behind him toward the bedroom wing of the house.

"David would never forgive me if I left you alone tonight. He thinks you hung the moon."

"But you walked on it."

He shot her a retiring look. "You're confusing me with Neil Armstrong. I've never even been to the moon. In here." He pulled her into a sumptuous bedroom that was so immaculate it did indeed look like no one had ever been in it. "Bathroom's through there. Take a shower. I'll fix you something to eat."

"I'm not hungry."

"Well, I am. Come on, Venus. Let's give the lady some privacy."

He went out, Venus tagging along behind his bare footsteps. Marnie pivoted slowly, getting her bearings. Sighing heavily, she realized she was actually glad Law had made up her mind for her. She was exhausted and a shower sounded marvelous.

The bathroom was as beautifully decorated as every other room in the house and had been designed with self-indulgence as a priority. The hot jets of the shower spouting from nozzles strategically mounted in all four corners massaged some of the fatigue from her body.

She dried off, briskly rubbed her hair with a fluffy towel, and slipped back into her clothes. Barefoot, she padded toward the kitchen, where Law was carrying on a conversation with Venus.

Seeing her out of the corner of his eye, he turned his head. "I was just asking Venus if you looked like a broad who would prefer mayonnaise or mustard."

"This broad prefers mustard."

"Good."

"The hot variety."

His eyebrows shot up. "Even better."

He liberally smeared two slices of French bread with spicy mustard and piled on slabs of ham and cheese. Before he was done, he had constructed two huge sandwiches with all the trimmings.

He straddled the seat of a chair and pointed her into another. He had changed from the wet swimsuit into a pair of cutoffs and a Naval Academy T-shirt. The casual attire made Marnie feel less self-conscious about her wet hair and bare feet.

"Beat it, Venus. You'll get the scraps." Tail drooping, the dog slunk into the corner. "David's spoiled her. He feeds her from the table."

Marnie attacked the food, though she didn't realize she was eating so ravenously until she caught Law smiling at her. "When's the last time you ate?"

"Last night. It's good," she said, nodding down at her plate. "Obviously you're very handy in the kitchen. You cleaned up mine better than I do."

"With David's help. We thought it was the least we could do after all the hard work you put into that birthday dinner."

She took a long drink of iced tea. "What, uh, what did you tell him about my disappearing act?" She was ashamed of her behavior now. Throwing a tantrum, then retreating upstairs seemed a childish and irrational stunt, though at the time she couldn't control it.

"I told him that you'd worked so hard on the party and were so emotionally overwrought, you'd had a crying jag and begged to be excused and left alone."

"And he believed you?"

"I made veiled references to 'that time of the month.' That ailment always carries with it a certain hush-hush, mysterious aura that effectively intimidates men from asking any more questions."

"How sexist."

"How true."

She frowned at him. "I don't usually throw fits even at that time of the month."

"Well, I exercised parental authority and didn't give him a chance to second-guess me. I began assigning KP chores. Before we left, he wanted to go upstairs and see about you, thank you for the dinner and new clothes, etcetera, but I told him that I had learned from vast experience that when a female is in that kind of mood, she's best left alone."

"You're right in one respect. Last night I was better left alone."

He reached across the table and laid his hand over hers. "About that damn car, Marnie."

"Never mind, Law."

"Uh-uh. I'm not going to let this fester until it becomes as painful as a boil. Had I known, I would *never* have spoiled your surprise."

"I didn't think it would be necessary to tell you what I was planning."

"I didn't buy the sports car as a lure. I swear that to you. I even thought you'd be excited for David." He gave a crooked smile. "I just wanted to do something very special for him."

"So did I!" she cried earnestly, splaying her hand on her chest.

"I understand and I'm sorry. It was bad judgment on my part. That's all I can say at this point, except"—he paused and gazed at her imploringly—"you've had him his whole life. You've been with him for fifteen other birthdays that I missed.

"Maybe I did go overboard by giving him that car. But don't condemn me for it before you think it through. I'm new at this. I'm bound to make a few mistakes. Be patient, okay?"

"Okay."

She felt very small, and very embarrassed for her behavior the night before, and very sleepy. In fact, she could barely hold her head up. When she focused her slumberous eyes on Law, he was watching her closely. "Did you give me something?" she asked on a burst of clarity.

"In your tea."

"You put a narcotic in my tea?"

"Not a narcotic. It's a little capsule that can't hurt you and will guarantee you a good night's sleep."

"Law!" She put all the strength she could muster behind the protest and it still sounded as weak as a new kitten's mewing.

He came around the table and scooped her out of her chair, lifting her against him. "Time for beddy-bye."

"I'll never forgive you for this," she mumbled against his chest. "No wonder you're so successful with women. You drug them first."

"Only the ones who give me a hassle." He set her down in front of the bathroom door. "Take your clothes off."

"That isn't necessary."

"It is unless you want me to take them off for you."

It was impossible to wage a war of wills when she couldn't even pull him into sharp focus. She relented and headed for the bathroom.

"There's a robe behind the door. I'll turn the bed down."

Somnambulistically she dropped her clothes on the floor as she peeled them off. The lightweight cotton robe was made for a man twice her size, but felt cool and soft against her skin. She overlapped it in front and loosely tied the belt at her waist.

By the time she returned to the bedroom, Law had the covers pulled back and was plumping up the pillows. "Good girl. In you go."

She lay down and he pulled the covers over her. Snuggling into the pillow, she closed her eyes. "I don't want to die a lonely, unhappy, embittered woman like my mother did, Law. I grieve more for her unhappiness than for her death."

"I know." He rubbed strands of her hair between his fingers. It wasn't quite dry yet and smelled like shampoo.

"I don't have any family left."

"Except for David."

"And I'm losing him."

"Not a chance." A tear slid from between her closed eyelids. He swept it from her cheek, then licked it off his thumb. "Want to hear a bedtime story?"

"As long as it has a happy ending."

"You be the judge."

"What's it about?"

"It's about this prince—a damned good-looking guy—who thought he had everything the world had to offer. He was flying high, literally and figuratively. A real cocky stud.

"Then one day he gets this letter in the mail, and it takes him to this modest house surrounded by flowers. The lady who lives there is toiling in the flower beds like a peasant. She has dirt on her knees and little dots of sweat on her upper lip. But she's not a peasant. She's really a princess in disguise.

"*She* doesn't know she's a princess, but everybody around her does because she's kind and compassionate and beautiful, with shiny dark hair and big gray eyes and a mouth . . . Lord, her mouth." He paused to contemplate the lips he was gently tracing with his fingertip.

"Anyway, the prince, after looking once into those big gray eyes and kissing that sweet, sweet mouth, thinks to himself, *Uh-oh, pal, you're sunk.* Typical of him, he starts behaving like a jerk, doing things like making unfounded accusations and issuing veiled threats and throwing wild orgies he doesn't even want to attend.

"The princess retaliates by putting this curse on him. She blinds him to all other women. He's about to die of terminal horniness, but the only woman he sees or wants is the princess.

"So he goes to this oracle and asks, 'What the hell am I going to do about this princess?' And the oracle says, 'For a prince, you're really stupid. Figure out a way to get her into your bed.' "

Law bent down to test Marnie's reaction to his unorthodox fairy tale. She had no reaction to it at all. She was sleeping.

16

Marnie sighed deeply before opening her eyes. Her body was languid with a lassitude as rich as heavy cream. It permeated every cell. Her heartbeats were strong and slow. She could almost feel the movement of her blood through her veins. She never remembered being this relaxed before. The inactivity was delicious.

Yawning, she stretched. That's when her foot brushed against another. She froze. Then, slowly, she turned to her other side.

Law was sleeping beside her. His blond hair was tousled and the lower half of his face was shadowed with stubble. The covers were pulled up only as far as his waist. His torso was bare.

Lying very still, hardly daring to breathe, Marnie studied him. Minutes ticked by. Her conscience told her to leave the bed while it was still safe. Then, when they next met eye to eye, they would do so with clear consciences and could pretend they hadn't shared a bed. But she was so tired of "safe" and couldn't force herself to move.

A ceiling fan was lazily circulating overhead. The droning hum of its motor was hypnotizing. It was still very early and only partially light in the bedroom.

So she allowed herself these few precious minutes in which to do exactly what she felt like doing rather than what her conscience dictated she should. Forcibly she tamped down all unpleasant thoughts about her mother's death or her uncertain future where David was concerned or her impossible love for this man who lay beside her.

How she loved him! And had since he first flashed her his killer grin and called her squirt.

"Good morning."

At first she thought his voice was a trick of her imagination. But then she saw his lips curve into that familiar smile. His eyes remained closed.

"What are you doing in bed with me, Law?"

"Getting hard."

She swallowed with such difficulty it was audible. "How long have you been here?"

"All night."

"All night? Sleeping?"

"Sleeping. Off and on, that is. Listening to you breathe. Watching you. Wanting to make love to you." He opened his eyes. They were brilliantly blue in the dim room. He smiled and gave a helpless little shrug. "Getting hard."

"How did you know I was awake?"

"I sensed it. You started breathing differently. Faster. Almost like you were aroused." He reached out and touched her pouty lips. "Are you?" he whispered huskily.

She only stared back at him, immersed in the hot blue fire of his eyes. Her tongue reflexively moistened the lips he was giving such close scrutiny. He groaned softly. "Are you, Marnie? Don't answer the way you think is proper or right. Tell me the truth. Are you aroused?"

She nodded before she answered out loud. No sooner had the sibilant word been spoken than Law leaned across the pillow and kissed her softly. At first he made brushing motions of his lips back and forth across hers. Then his tongue tickled the center of her upper lip. Her body reflexively inclined forward.

His hand curved around the back of her neck and drew her head closer. The kiss he gave her was soft and deep and wet. His tongue sank into her mouth. Instinctively she raised her hands, laying them on his chest. The crisp, curly hair felt delightful against her fingertips. She played with it curiously, tweaking clumps of it between her fingers.

He kissed the corner of her lips like a refrain, a benediction, then pulled back to gaze into her eyes. Shyly Marnie withdrew her hands. "Are you ready to stop, Marnie?" She shook her head no. Law stared at her intently as he slowly bicycled his legs to remove the covers.

Her eyes skittered downward and registered wordless astonishment.

"I wasn't kidding, was I?" he asked.

"No, you weren't."

"What are you going to do about it?"

"I'm not sure."

"Think about it." He took her hand, planted a fervent kiss in the palm, then laid it over his sex. He gave a soft, masculine grunt of pleasure. "Take your time."

His eyes turned dark and he grimaced with supreme satisfaction as she grazed the velvety tip with her thumb. "Ah, Marnie." Moments later, chest rising and falling rapidly, he groaned, "Goody-Two-Shoes, my foot."

He rolled her to her back and leaned above her, fumbling with the knotted belt of the robe she wore. When it came undone, he impatiently pushed the cloth aside.

His haste was immediately checked. He sucked in a sharp, shocked breath. His eyes moved over her nakedness greedily, hungrily. His expression was wearing a question mark when his eyes finally moved up to her face. "You grew up real good, squirt."

Starting at her shoulders, his hand explored its way down her arm, charting each vein in the back of her hand before moving across her chest, pausing to fondle her breast, then down her belly. He lightly ground the heel of his hand over the feathery triangle of hair before caressing her slender thighs in turn.

His touch elicited a million delicious tingles along her skin. She couldn't remain still. Her throat and back arched in response when his fingers lightly skimmed her belly; she flexed her knees when his hand glided over her hip. For once she felt an obligation only to her body and its erotic responses to Law's caresses.

"You're so beautiful," he whispered. "I don't know what to kiss first."

He decided on her mouth while his thumb mischievously finessed her nipple erect. With his lips still wet from the passion of their kiss, he pressed them against her breast. She dug her fingers in his hair and gasped his name.

"Does that mean yes or no?"

"Yes," she moaned, "yes."

The very tip of his tongue nudged the very tip of her breast, flicking it repeatedly, lightly. Marnie uttered a sound close to a sob.

"More?"

"Yes."

He sipped her nipple between his lips and sucked it with gentle ardency. The stroking heat of his tongue and tugging motion of his mouth touched off an erotic explosion inside her. Up till then she had never known what an impact lovemaking could have on her entire being. She became greedy to have all of him.

He responded to her urgent prompting and settled himself between her thighs. Her creamy warmth enveloped him. He gave a glad murmur and thrust forward.

The tip of his organ barely touched her, barely glanced that precious spot, but that was more than sufficient. All the love and desire she had felt for him concentrated there and manifested itself into a shattering climax.

It spun through her body like a cyclone. She felt it in her belly and breasts. Dizzily it whirled through her system until it reached her very fingertips. Its effects continued to sparkle and sizzle long after the crisis had passed.

Finally she opened her eyes and gazed at Law, stunned by the immensity of sensation he had evoked from a body she'd never considered voluptuous. "I'm sorry."

He threw back his head and laughed out loud. "For what? For being one of the sexiest women ever created? God, you're amazing," he whispered as he whisked a kiss across her mouth. "Wonderful and amazing."

"You're embarrassing me." Her whole body felt flushed and feverish, a heat enhanced by the carnal way his eyes and hands and lips were moving over it, sampling tastes and textures.

"You've got the most sensitive nipples." His voice was hushed with admiration and awe.

"They're disproportionately large," she mumbled, half-heartedly trying to deflect his fondling hands.

"Is that why they always look erect?"

"They don't!"

"Oh, yes, they do, squirt."

His use of the pet name had surprised them both. "That's the second time you've called me that. I wasn't sure you even remembered."

"I didn't until I started making love to you."

"Why then?"

"I guess I remember watching you on the beach one day and thinking what a knockout you promised to be in a few years." His fingertips fanned her nipples lightly. "I remember regretting that I wouldn't be around to see you turn into a woman. Selfishly I'm glad that dumb son of a bitch broke your heart."

"What dumb son of a bitch?"

"The one you loved. The one who threw you over."

"Oh," she said in a small voice.

"If it weren't for him, you wouldn't be available." He lowered his head and kissed one rosy nipple. "I must be living right."

He continued to kiss his way down her body, disregarding her breathless protests as his mouth moved closer to the top of her thighs.

"Law," she whimpered as he parted them.

He nuzzled her affectionately, then kissed her, tasting her recent sweet release against his lips. His nimble tongue swirled and dipped and stroked and teased until she was once again on the brink of delirium.

Law levered himself above her, poised to enter. "Marnie, this has been a long time coming. Open your eyes and look at me."

She not only opened her eyes but looped her arms around his neck. With a long, deep groan, he sheathed himself inside her. For a moment he was still, breathing unsteadily as he gazed into her face.

"Aren't you going to . . . ?"

"Not yet," he said quietly against the corner of her mouth. "Your mouth is so provocative."

"It is?"

"Hmm. Sometime I'll tell you about the fantasies I've had about it."

"Tell me now."

"No."

"Why not?"

"You'd be embarrassed and I don't want to come yet. I will if I talk about that."

He tipped her head back and kissed her. Then, moving his hands down her body and clasping her tightly around the waist, he lifted her into the cradle of his hips and began to stroke her.

It was Venus's tentative scratching that woke Marnie up the second time. Physically spent, she and Law had fallen asleep. Her limbs were hopelessly entangled with his. He had one hand possessively covering her breast and the other ensnared in her hair. When she tried to extricate herself, he mumbled grouchily, "Lie still."

"I need to get up. Besides, Venus needs to go outside."

"That bitch," he grumbled, rolling to his back and kicking off the sheet. "I'll let her out and make some coffee." He hooked Marnie around the neck and gave her a sound, tongue-thrusting kiss. "Save my place." Releasing her, he threw his legs over the side of the bed and headed for the bedroom door, unmindful of his nakedness.

Marnie wasn't unmindful of it. She lay amid the hopelessly twisted sheets and admired him until he was out of sight. Her body all but glowed with the smug knowledge that she had the most beautiful lover in the whole universe.

Making her way into the bathroom, she noticed that her body had undergone drastic changes since the night before. There were whisker burns on her breasts and stomach. An ache that was more pleasure than pain resided between her thighs. She relished these ravages.

After taking a quick shower, she dressed. Carrying her shoes, she made her way through the house, going in the general direction of the kitchen. A partially opened door caught her eye. She gave it a slight push and it swung open.

David's room. That much was immediately apparent. Clothes had been strewn around, a bad habit that had once irritated her and that now she found poignant and endearing. Posters of rock stars, sports heroes, and one of a bikini-clad, radiant model adorned the walls. A scale model of the *Victory* stood on the desk, where there was also a stack of schoolbooks.

For him to have inhabited it such a short time, the room had his indelible stamp on it. In addition to his familiar possessions there was also a new TV with a built-in VCR, something he'd wanted for a long time. A telephone that looked recently installed was on the nightstand. His boom box had a stack of new cassette tapes beside it.

Tears clouded Marnie's eyes as she backed out of the room, pulling the door closed. She hadn't realized the extent of Law's generosity. This house must seem like paradise to David, who had been taught, mainly out of necessity, that material possessions weren't important.

She must get him back right away. Otherwise he might be lost to her forever. As soon as she saw him, she would demand that he move home, where he belonged.

Law had pulled on a pair of gym shorts. He was in the kitchen, shaking a carafe of orange juice when she went in. "Coffee's almost ready."

"I don't want any coffee." Her curt tone of voice arrested the vigorous movement of the carafe. "The only thing I want from you is a full explanation for the fancy toys you've lavished on David. I thought we had settled the issue of your extravagances last night."

With carefully controlled motions, he set down the carafe. "Was I supposed to take back what I'd already given him? Be reasonable, Marnie. What we settled last night was that I was an indulgent parent because I haven't had my son for sixteen years and that you were going to be patient with me."

"Well, after looking into that wonderland of electronics passing as a bedroom, my patience just ran out."

He propped his hands on his hips. "What brought this on so suddenly?"

"You're showering David with goodies to seduce him away from me!" she accused him.

"That's not true."

"I think it is."

"Why would I do that?"

"Because you've got to be first in everybody's book. Top gun. The champion. A-number-one. On top."

"Less than an hour ago," he drawled, "you were on top. And loving every minute of it. Or should I say every inch of it?"

She went hot all over with rage and embarrassment. Dropping her shoes onto the floor, she worked her feet into them. Spinning on the heels, she marched toward the front door. She yanked it open only to be confronted by Venus and David on their way inside.

"Mom!" he exclaimed. "I couldn't believe it when I saw your car out front. What's going on?"

She was so startled to see him, she couldn't speak a word. She was also afraid that something in her appearance would reveal what she had been doing for the last few hours in Law's bed.

"It's your grandmother, David," Law said from behind her.

Marnie finally found her voice and quietly informed him, "She died yesterday afternoon."

"Yesterday?"

"Marnie and I discussed it and decided not to ruin your party. I'll leave you two alone. Come on, Venus. Let's go out back."

The dog followed Law from the hallway, leaving Marnie

and David by themselves. He was filled with remorse. "Gee, Mom, I'm sorry I wasn't around when it happened."

"You couldn't have known."

"Yeah, but you were by yourself last night."

"I—it was all right. I needed some time to think anyway."

David stepped forward and hugged her. "You must feel awful. I know how I'd feel if anything happened to you."

She wrapped her arms around him and held him close. Tears streamed down her cheeks. "Thank you, darling."

"When's the funeral?" he asked, stepping back.

"Later today. I saw no reason to delay it. She had made all the arrangements beforehand. Of course we already had the cemetery plot," she added, thinking of the graves of Sharon and her father.

"Dad and I'll be there. What time?"

She told him. "It'll be a brief service." He nodded, shaking loose several strands of blond hair. Reflexively she reached up to smooth them back. "Did you enjoy the party?"

"It was awesome. We stayed up till four playing poker."

"Poker?"

"Yeah, Dad gave me some pointers before I left and I ended up winning ten bucks."

"I didn't even know about the party."

"I tried to call yesterday and ask permission. Now I know why you weren't home. For a while I was afraid Dad wasn't going to let me go."

"Why not?"

"He wanted to know if Jack's parents would be home and if there would be any booze or drugs or anything like that. I had to convince him that Jack was straight and so was everybody invited. He said he believed me but called Mrs. Moore anyway." He grinned. "Now I've got *two* strict parents!"

"Is Law strict with you?"

"We've got what he calls rules of the house. No TV until all homework is finished and he's checked over it. Only one soda per day, but I get all the fresh fruit juice I can hold. Telephone calls are limited to three a night and only fifteen minutes each. If the boom box is loud enough for him to hear, it's too loud.

"He's a lot like you, Mom. He even told me I couldn't lie around on my butt all summer, but had to get a job if I wanted gas money. See? He agrees with you about that. I told him I was planning on working anyway."

"Do you like living with him, David?" She knew it was unfair of her to put him on the spot, but her earnest expression demanded a truthful answer.

"Well, sure," he replied, gesturing awkwardly. "It's a great house. I'd be real lonesome without Venus now, I'm so used to having her around. After dinner every night Dad and I talk about stuff, just like you and I do. Sometimes we crack jokes and laugh, but he gets serious about subjects like God and having integrity, things that really matter, you know?"

He covered a huge yawn. "Gosh, I'm sorry, Mom. Last night is catching up with me."

"Why don't you take a nap? I'll see you later this afternoon."

"Are you sure? Don't you want me to come home with you?"

"No, I'll be fine. You rest."

She could tell he was relieved, though he gave her another sincere hug. She was already out the front door when she heard him call out "Hey, Dad? Where are you?" much the way he used to greet her.

How could she compete with his natural father, who was an astronaut, who could afford to give him a new car and a new TV, when she had been trying for more than a year to afford new wallpaper for his room?

She couldn't. She wouldn't. Not any longer.

17

Marnie trudged up the stairs of her house. She didn't turn on any lights, although it was already dusk and violet shadows filled every corner.

In her bedroom she stepped out of her black leather pumps and laid her handbag on top of the bureau. Crossing to the window that overlooked the backyard, she gazed at nothing for several minutes. Despair had immobilized her.

Just as she was about to turn away, she spotted David's soccer ball lying forgotten beneath the azalea bushes. It looked lonely, discarded, and deserted, and seemed to represent all the sadness in her life.

With a heavy sigh she reached behind her for the zipper of her black dress.

"Let me do that for you."

She jumped, then spun around. Law was standing in the open doorway, still dressed in his dark suit and white shirt.

When her heart had returned to its normal place, she repri-
manded him. "You scared me half to death. Where'd you
come from?"

"We followed you home."

"We? Where's David?"

"I sent him to my house. He didn't want to go, but I told
him that our conversation was for adults only and that he
wasn't invited."

"What conversation?"

"The one we're about to have. First I want to know how
you're holding up."

"You mean in regard to my mother?" He nodded. "I'm
at peace because I know she is. At last."

"Good. Before we commence, let's get you out of that
dress." He moved into the room. "Turn around."

"I'm not going to take my dress off, Law. If we're going
to talk, I'd rather keep it on."

He appeared disinclined to argue. "Suit yourself, but
I'm going to get out of a few things." He took off his jacket
and tie and tossed both across the end of her bed. He un-
buttoned his collar button and rolled up his cuffs. "There.
Much better."

"I'm glad you're here, actually," she told him. "I need to
talk to you too."

"Shoot."

"You go first."

"Okay." He propped his hands on his hips, took a deep
breath, and stared at the floor between his feet for several

seconds before lifting his eyes to hers. "David and I have discussed this, Marnie."

"Discussed what?"

"We want to go to court and have his name legally changed to Kincaid."

The words went through her like a spear. She almost cried out in agony. Having David's name changed would make it final. It would cement his identity. He would be Law's son. Not hers.

"I see," she croaked.

"I want to publicly acknowledge him."

"You don't have to, Law. The public disclosure my mother threatened you with will never happen."

"I know, but public disclosure seems unimportant now. In fact, I want everybody to know who he is and how much he means to me. I called my parents this morning and told them about him."

"What did they say?"

He shook his head with chagrin. "You mean once the shock wore off? They're rushing down next weekend to meet their grandson. He talked to both of them and ran up a hell of a long distance bill. I think it's love."

Marnie, feeling choked up, gave him her back and moved to the window again. "That's wonderful. I'm so glad for David's sake." Her pause lasted for the span of several heartbeats. "In light of that news, it's a good thing I've reached some conclusions of my own."

Her narrow shoulders lifted as she took a deep breath. "I

won't fight you in a custody battle, Law. In the first place, I couldn't compete. You're his natural father. Your credibility speaks for itself. I've been an excellent parent, but so far you seem to be doing an excellent job of it yourself, which, I confess, surprises me.

"In the second place, I wouldn't put David in a position of having to choose between us. He loves me. He loves you. I believe we both love him and want what's best. He's happy living with you. He wants your name. I think it would be best if he went to live with you permanently. I intend to tell him that."

Her throat was achy and tight with emotion. She could barely squeeze the words out. "In two years he'll be going off to college anyway."

She bowed her head. "I haven't been entirely unselfish, you see. From the day Sharon told me she was pregnant, I wanted the baby because I wanted someone to love, someone who would love me back. A child that I took care of would love me instinctively.

"Sharon monopolized my parents' attention even if it was negative attention. She exhausted them. They had very little energy to devote to me. So I needed David as much as he needed me."

She looked at Law over her shoulder. "But he doesn't need me to take care of him any longer. And I can't burden him with the responsibility of making me happy, fulfilling my needs. I won't."

"I feel constrained to interrupt," Law said. "Aren't you being just a little rough on yourself?"

"I'm not trying to sound like a martyr. Don't think I see myself like that. I spent all day preparing this speech. Every word is heartfelt. Please let me finish. There's something else." He inclined his head, indicating that she should continue.

"What happened this morning . . ."

"Hmm?"

"There are several reasons why it happened."

"Good foreplay for one."

"Law, please."

"Sorry." He gave an impatient wave of his hand.

"I felt so awful after Mother died. Hopeless, you know. Like wondering what good is life if it ends so pitifully sad anyway?"

"I understand. You needed contact with another human being, and affirmation that life might just be worth living."

"Yes," she said, vaguely surprised that he understood so well and was able to articulate what she was feeling. "That's precisely it. And—"

"There's more?"

"The situation caught me at a very emotional time."

"You were seeking an outlet for your emotions. The outlet that presented itself was sex, the ultimate emotional and physical catharsis."

"Exactly," she said softly.

"Is that all?" he asked, moving toward her.

"Yes."

"Liar."

Her head snapped up. "What?"

"You're lying. There's another reason that you had sex with me." He tilted her chin up with his crooked finger. "You love me. Don't you, Marnie?" She swallowed, wet her lips, and blinked. "Don't you?" he repeated.

She closed her eyes and nodded her head.

"I was the dumb son of a bitch who broke your heart."

"You didn't break my heart on purpose," she said, opening her tearful eyes. "You just made it impossible for me to love any other man. Even I couldn't have known that a teenage crush would endure this long."

She felt a seventeen-year-old burden being lifted off her heart. The freedom to speak her love for him out loud was well worth the price of some pride.

"I have always loved you. When you were rolling around on the beach blanket with my sister. When you were being launched into space. When you came storming up my sidewalk, furious over the anonymous letters. I have always loved you, Law Kincaid."

He slid his arms around her and pulled her close. "Marnie, my dear Marnie, it took longer to catch up to me, but I love you like hell." He bent his head and kissed her forehead beneath her bangs. When he pulled back, however, he was frowning.

"That was quite a speech you made, but about three

fourths of it was crap. David wouldn't think of leaving you and coming to live with me permanently. He's told me that repeatedly and unconditionally. In fact, it wouldn't surprise me if he's packing to come home right now.

"Another thing is that I never thought you were a martyr. You're certainly not selfish. In fact, you're about the least selfish person I've ever met. You have a huge capacity for loving, which I plan to cash in on." He brushed his lips across hers.

"And if you had let me finish *my* speech before you started *yours*, you would have learned that David isn't the only Hibbs I want to change into a Kincaid."

"What?"

"I figure a name change and a marriage could be handled by one judge. We'd be killing two birds with one stone. It would entail only one trip to the courthouse, and since parking space downtown is at a premium—"

"Law!"

"What?"

"You want to get married? To me?"

"Of course to you. You're going to be the mother of all future little Kincaids." He splayed one hand over her stomach and slid it down to cover her lower body. "In fact, since I broke my own golden rule with you and didn't take any precautions, there might be one already nesting inside you."

He kissed her softly and left his lips against hers when he added, "The last time I failed to use a condom I scored big, so I want to hustle you to the altar as soon as possible. I'd like for my other babies to have the advantages, like legitimacy, that David missed."

He covered her breasts, his thumbs seeking out their centers and making them stiff with seductive strokes. "I want to watch you feed our children."

"Law." She laid her hands against his cheeks and spoke his beloved name in a wondrous whisper.

Angling his head, he kissed her with no restraint. She locked her arms around his neck as her tongue actively mated with his, exhibiting the sensuality she'd been born with but which had been reserved exclusively for him.

"Here are the rules of the house," he said gruffly, ending the kiss while he still had the control to think. "You'll go on being your wonderful self. I'll become a faithful but awfully horny husband."

"Suzette and clones will have to go."

"Agreed. Besides, none can hold a candle to you when you get prone between a set of sheets." His smile gradually relaxed and his eyes peered seriously into hers. "The only thing I can't give up, Marnie, is my work. If I couldn't fly, I wouldn't be Law. If I weren't Law, you wouldn't love me. Okay?"

"Okay."

"It'll get scary," he continued in that same serious tone. "The families go through pure hell during a shuttle mission. I've seen it cause nervous breakdowns. I've seen it tear up marriages."

"Other marriages don't have me," she said with a confident toss of her head. "I'm tough. And I have infinite patience. Look how long I had to wait for you."

His eyes turned dark with passion. "I know the feeling." He adjusted his body along hers, leaving no doubt in her mind what was coming next, and reached around her for her zipper. "Now can we finally get you out of this dress?"

About the Author

SANDRA BROWN began her writing career in 1980. After selling her first book, she wrote a succession of romance novels under several pseudonyms, most of which remain in print. She has become one of the country's most popular novelists, earning the notice of Hollywood and of critics. More than fifty of her books have appeared on the *New York Times* bestseller list. There are seventy million copies of her books in print, and her work has been translated into thirty languages. Prior to writing, she worked in commercial television as an on-air personality for *PM Magazine* and local news in Dallas. She and her husband now divide their time between homes in Texas and South Carolina.